The Rainbow's End

Nurse Hal Among The Amish

Book 2

Fay Risner

Cover Art
Picture by Fay Risner
All Rights Reserved 2018

Copyright © 2018
All Rights Reserved Revised Edition
Author Fay Risner

ISBN 13 978 0982459522
ISBN 10 0982459521

Booksbyfay Publisher
Author Fay Risner
Editor Kay Holst
Nursing Consultant Tracy Hanson RN

This book is dedicated to Kay Holst for doing the editing. Her diligent effort to find all the errors I made was very much appreciated by me. Between us we have made a smoother, easier reading product for readers. I thank her for her help.

I have set my rainbow in the clouds, and it will be the sign of the covenant between me and the earth. Whenever I bring clouds over the earth and the rainbow appears in the clouds, I will remember my covenant between me and you and all living creatures of every kind. Never again will the waters become a flood to destroy all life.

Genesis 9:13-14

Chapter 1

esuoH eeffoC yellA avaJ. Those six inch black letters arched in a horseshoe shape on the cafe's large, plate glass window. Underneath them thick, wavy, painted fingers of steam rose out of a delicate, white, china coffee cup. The steam swirled its way up toward the letters. Hallie Lindstrom's eyes lit on the words as she slid into the red cushioned booth. She wondered how the owner came up with the name Java Alley Coffee House. Not that she found anything wrong with the name, but the cafe sat in the middle of a row of buildings just off Main Street. No alley near it except the back one that the delivery trucks used. Hal had never known that one or any other alley in Wickenburg, Iowa to have a name.

She ducked her head to peer under the advertising so she could look up and down the street. She glanced at her watch. Her boss, Barb Sloan, should have shown up by now. She said she would close the Home Health Office at noon and meet here for lunch. It was already twelve twenty. Doesn't take very long to drive across this small town. Not much traffic any time of day and especially not at noon when everyone stops to eat. Hal had other things to do after lunch. She hated wasting time waiting for Barb.

Impatiently, she leaned back and stared at the ceiling while she drummed the table with her fingers. A dark brown splotch on the ceiling tile at the fan's base indicated a roof leak. The fan blades turned hypnotically slow.

The air flow was just enough to keep a fly from lighting anywhere close to the blades. The insect was persistent, leaving and coming right back to try to light in the brown spot again.

Hal looked around the room. Coffee always smelled better to her than it tasted. The different scents coming from the dozen coffee pots lined up behind the counter co-mingled together – hazelnut, French vanilla, southern pecan, and a variety of other flavors. She was thinking she should get the waitress's attention and at least order a cup of coffee when she saw Barb hustling across the room.

"I just about gave up on you," Hal said.

Breathless from rushing, Barb pushed her straight, brown, shoulder length hair away from her face and wheezed, "Had a last minute prospective client come in the office. Slowed me down, but I'm here now. Let's order. The minute I get a whiff of this place I've got to have a cup of flavored coffee." Barb waved at a waitress.

Shirley Graham, age sixty, hustled toward them. Her silvery blonde hairdo was plastered around her face by a red baseball cap adorned with a big white C on it. Dressed in a black turtleneck sweater covered by a pink cardigan with black slacks, she wore black, tied, sensible shoes. Her small cross earrings matched a cross dangling from a fragile, gold chain necklace.

No customer could accuse Shirley of having a favorite sports team. She had a variety of sports caps in colors to match many of her outfits. Older than most of the waitresses, she held her own at the job. Shirley had been working long enough to be appreciated by her customers.

Order book out in front of her and pen poised, she asked briskly, "How's the day going for you two ladies?"

Hal smiled. "We're fine."

"But starved and thirsty," added Barb.

"What can I get you, Sweetie?"

"I want a toasted cheese and ham sandwich and vanilla

2

coffee," Barb ordered.

Shirley shifted her weight and peered down her nose at Hal. "I'll take the same except I want hazelnut coffee."

"Be back in a jiffy, ladies." Shirley wheeled and headed for the kitchen. The sway of her cross earrings caught the light and flashed as she walked, warning everyone to get out of her way. She had an order to fill.

Barb leaned her elbows on the table and concentrated on Hal.

"Now while we're waiting for our food, fill me in on your love life. I've been dying to find out."

"Boy, you get right to the point. Nothing much to tell. This morning, John and some neighbors started building a clinic room on the side of the house. Soon Amish people can come to our home to let me treat them. I doubt I get much business, but it may be the best way I have of proving I can be a productive member of their society so I get accepted by the Amish community," Hal said honestly. "I have to be accepted. It would make it hard on John and his children if I'm not."

Barb had a perplexed look in her hazel eyes. "The pay won't be very good from Amish patients. You realize that?"

"I know that," Hal admitted. "In fact, there isn't any pay. I will just be doing my share to help others."

"In that case, don't you think you better keep working a full schedule for the Home Health Department? You're one of the best nurses I have. I hate the fact that you're cutting back."

Hal shook her head. "No, I can't be two places at once. The Amish community needs to know they can count on me being home in the afternoons."

"Here you go, Sweeties," Shirley said when she set the coffee cups in front of them.

Waiting until the waitress departed, Barb pushed her cup over and leaned on the table to ask, "When's the wedding?"

As Hal fingered the rim of her steaming coffee, the scent of hazelnut rose from the cup. She didn't look up when she answered, "Don't know."

3

"I suppose you have been too busy to set a date?" Barb suggested, eying her.

"Not exactly."

Puzzlement crossed Barb's face. "Then what exactly?"

Hal sighed. "John hasn't brought the wedding up since he asked me to marry him," she admitted reluctantly.

"Don't you think you should bring it up to him? It takes lots of planning for a wedding. You need to know what your deadline is," Barb insisted.

"Perhaps I should."

Barb looked concerned. "Mr. Lapp hasn't changed his mind, has he? He isn't expecting you to just be a live-in nurse among other things?"

"No!" Hal expelled adamantly. "I'm sure he wants to marry me."

"Good. Am I going to be invited to the wedding?"

Hal giggled. "I'll make sure you are."

"Keep in mind, maybe you don't need much notice, but I do. I have to get a new dress," Barb teased.

Laughing, Hal said, "Noted."

After lunch, Hal was on the outskirts of town and coming up to Earnie Long's repair garage and gas station. She decided to pull in and get a can of Cherry Coke. Earnie's feet were sticking out from under a car in the garage. Hal walked to the overhead door and said, "Hey, Earnie, it's Hal Lindstrom. I just want a can of pop. I can leave my money on the counter if you don't want to stop what you're doing."

Earnie, his receding strawberry red hairline smeared with grease, wheeled out from under the car on a trolley. He gave her an oil smudged smile. "Knock yourself out, my girl."

Hal grinned back at him. "Thanks."

The last business, she past was the Kent feed store. That place always seemed to do a good business. If you went by the number of pickups in the parking lot. Outside of town was the tree nursery. From the look of the front lot, the nursery had just gotten in a new shipment to add to the choices that grew in the fields behind the building. In large black pots, a variety of

4

skinny fruit trees, redbuds, flowering cherries and maples had sparse, bare limbs reaching skyward. Colorado Blue Spruce, Douglas fir, and arborvitae, in various sizes mingled, with rose of Sharon, honeysuckle and privet hedge shrubs.

Once Hal was on the highway, she took in the rolling hills of southern Iowa. Oaks, cottonwoods, dogwoods and plum limbs swelled with buds. Weeping willows had turned yellow-green. The season's birth was everywhere. Newborn calves and lambs frolicked across the pastures alongside their mothers. With the changing of the seasons, she felt an excitement and joy. It was so good to be able to enjoy the scenery not covered in a coating of white.

She traveled these country roads almost every day. As she watched the now familiar scenery she sped past, she had a comforting sense she was headed for home. A feeling she hadn't experienced since she left her parents farm near Titonka, Iowa.

She turned off the pavement onto the gravel and headed west. Her mind raced over the last few months. How quickly she became involved with the Lapp family. Suddenly, her conversation with Barb played over in her head. The questions Barb put to her worried her. Though she would never tell her friend that. Why hadn't John brought up a wedding date? When she was at the Lapp farm she certainly felt like part of the family. She was sure that John loved her enough to marry her. Almost sure anyway. Emma, Noah and Daniel had accepted her. She loved them as if they were her own children. She was sure the Lapp children felt the same way about her.

Never the less, this was not going to be an easy union with all the hurtles faced by an English woman marrying an Amish man. Hal knew nothing about Amish ways. She certainly hadn't made it easy on John to get used to her. From the moment they met, she'd made one mistake after another. Things that would have made any sane English man have enough doubts about her to cause him to back off. Heaven knows why John Lapp fell in love with her. However, she was certainly glad that he did, because she loved him with her

5

whole heart.

Hal slowed down to turn into the Lapp driveway. Attached to the post below the mailbox was a sign she hadn't noticed before. Emma must have put it up that morning. It read, All things Are Open Before God.

A bare square of dirt in the lawn along side the ditch was noticeable now that the snow had melted. A row of gallon milk jugs had been stuck in the dirt. Hal made a mental note to ask Emma what that was all about. In front of the barn were two buggies with horses attached. Hal noted that all Amish horses were as alike as Amish clothes, always red with dark red manes and tails.

The sound of hammers drew her attention to the house. She marveled at how the new room was going up so fast. Two men, John and a boy, up on ladders, nailed the framework to the rafters. A heavy set farmer, short legged with a ruddy, round face, turned to look as she slowed down. The other man, about John's age, was tall and lanky. The boy was around Emma's age.

Out of the corner of her eyes, Hal saw a low flying, black and white blur spring out of the ditch and rush toward her car. Her heart pounded as she skid to a stop. Patches, the Lapp dog, reared up and put his front paws on the door. He peered in at her, whining a greeting. Giving the window a lick with his long, juicy tongue, he showed her he was glad to see her. Hal pressed hard on the button and lowered her spit smeared window. She snapped, "Patches, get down."

The dog did as he was told. He loped ahead of her up the driveway and sat down to wait for her. Hal hated that he had started coming out on the road to greet her. She wanted the Lapp children to continue to like her. Running over their dog would definitely put a damper on their feelings for her. Besides, she was fond of Patches. No way did she want something to happen to the feisty pet.

Hal started her car and slowly halted in front of the house. Her face flushed when she noticed the Amish men twisted on the ladders to watch her. It crossed her mind that it sure would be easier for her if she could morph herself into an Amish woman whenever she needed to and slip quietly by those men. First impressions were important right now. What the men saw was a curly, copper-red mop of hair on a bright blue-eyed English woman clothed in a bright green blouse and blue jeans. Her buggy happened to be a gaudy, copper sedan. Nothing about her spelled demur or plain. Some time soon, she would have to tone down in order to get the Amish community's approval before John announced he was going to marry her. Maybe the way she looked was the reason for John's slowness to discuss their wedding. If it was, she wished he would say so instead of her having to drag it out of him.

Wagging his tail, Patches jumped on her and licked her chin the minute she stepped out of the car.

"I know you're glad to see me, but you really shouldn't be out on the road," Hal scolded.

The dog took her tone of voice to heart. He put his skinny, long tail between his legs and slinked off to hide behind the maple tree. From his safe place, he peeked around the trunk and watched her.

"Gute afternoon," John called, waving from his ladder.

"Good afternoon." Hal waved back.

"Stay there. I am coming down," John told her.

He climbed down the ladder and walked across the yard. Hal's heart beat faster as she watched the bushy-bearded Amish farmer, wearing a straw hat over his dark brown hair, come to meet her. He had a ready boyish smile on his face.

John stopped right in front of her, stuck his hands in his pockets and asked softly, "How did your day go?"

"It was good. I just had lunch with Barb Sloan." She brought her hand up to pat his shoulder then dropped it by her side. No touching allowed as long as the neighbors were watching.

"Gute," John replied, watching her lower her hand. His dark chocolate eyes sparked mischievously. Somehow, he always managed to read her mind.

"You certainly have been working hard today. I

7

couldn't imagine how much you'd have done already," Hal marveled, listening to the hammers pound nails.

"We start early when we have a building to put up. It's time to stop for a break. Will you ask Emma to bring us something cold to drink?" With a warm twinkle in his dark eyes, he caressed her chin with a finger. "I can do that," Hal responded, returning his gaze as she pushed his finger away. "But you probably shouldn't do that." She whispered and nodded toward the men.

The short man looked over his shoulder. In a breezy, crackling voice, he said, "John Lapp, as long as you are down, bring us some more nails. We are about out."

Without taking his eyes off Hal, John responded, "Be right there, Elton." In a lowered voice, he asked, "Do you think we could go for a walk alone after supper tonight?"

"I'd like that," Hal whispered. "Now don't hold up progress. Get the men their nails. I'll see to the drinks."

Whatever Emma fixed for lunch sure left a delectable smell throughout the house. Hal wondered with regret what good foods she missed. Stopping in the kitchen doorway, she watched John's fifteen-year-old daughter sweep crumbs from under the table. As she moved the broom back and forth in swift motions, the girl's white prayer cap-strings, dangling down her back, brushed back and forth along her shoulders.

She was changing from a teenager to a young woman. She had grown an inch taller just in the short time Hal had known her. Anyone would be blind not to notice that she had filled out. The girl seemed to have overcome the depressed moods that worried Hal when they first met. Now she was cheerful and sure of herself.

John's daughter was turning into a beauty. Her soft, brown hair was neatly tucked under her head covering. With a long, slender nose and freckles splashed across her tanned cheeks, she was the picture perfect country girl. Emma's feature that Hal loved most was her lovely, gray-green eyes. Not that she would ever ask John or Emma, but Hal often wondered if Emma's eye coloring was inherited from her mother. Not only the eyes, Hal imagined were like Diane Lapp's, but the rest of the girl's pretty looks as well. As curious as she was about what John's wife had looked like, Hal knew Diane was a subject left well enough alone in the Lapp household.

"Hello. About got the kitchen work done?" Hal looked around the spotless kitchen. A line of cast iron skillets hung on nails over the work counter topped with white Formica speckled with blue. She walked across the shiny, black and white checked linoleum to the mudroom and unhooked the dustpan from the wall. Bending in front of Emma, she waited for the girl to sweep the pile of dirt into the pan. After she emptied the dustpan out the back door, Hal sat down at the long wooden table in the middle of the kitchen.

"Just about," Emma replied, putting a stack of plates in the dish cupboard.

Hal put her elbows on the table and rested her chin on her hands. "Your father wants to know if you can bring the men something to drink."

"I fixed some lemonade. Want a glass?" Emma said, setting glasses on the counter.

"Homemade lemonade sounds good. My mother used to make it that way. Will you join me? You must need a break by now," Hal suggested.

"We can take ours out in the yard and sit with the men," Emma said.

Suddenly, Hal felt jittery about facing the Amish strangers. She asked, "Do you think that will be all right?"

"Jah, it is about time Plain people get to know you, Hallie." Emma said briskly as she poured the lemonade. "Help me carry the glasses."

As Hal and Emma headed for the shade of the maple tree, the girl called, "Come get a glass while it is still cold."

The men climbed down the ladders. After he tossed his straw hat on the ground, the short man sat down in the grass. He joked, "You do not have to tell me twice. I am thirsty."

Emma handed him a glass. She gave one of the two she had to the boy and sat next to him. Hal gave the other man and John a glass then got down beside John.

"Nurse Hal, I want you to meet Elton Bontrager, Luke Yoder and his son Levi," John introduced, pointing at each of them.

Elton, close to sixty, wore a dark blue shirt and faded, thin pants. A patch had been put in the straddle to make the pants last longer. Hal wondered how an industrious Amish farmer wore out the straddle of his pants before he did the knees. The short man gave her a wide grin as he shook her hand. "Gute to meet you."

"Gute to meet you," said Luke, holding out his hand. He was a good-looking man with yellow hair and a beard the color of corn.

Levi was a younger version of his father. He nodded bashfully at her and lowered his bright blue eyes to the ground.

Eldon took a sip from his glass. He glanced over at Hal and cleared his throat before he spoke. "It is nice of you to make this clinic available for Plain people."

"I appreciate you building the clinic for me. This room will be a useful addition to the house to help with medical aid in the Amish community," Hal assured him. It passed through her mind that she had heard his name somewhere before, but she was fairly certain she'd never met him.

Levi said softly to Emma, "I hear the best laying flock in the county you have. What is your secret?"

Emma blushed. "Nah secret."

Levi persisted with interest. "What kind of hens are they?"

"Don't know," Emma said. "Want to come look at my chickens? I will introduce you to my pet rooster."

"Jah, I would like to see them. You have a pet rooster?" Levi scoffed as if he didn't believe her.

Emma opened her mouth to speak but realized the grownups weren't talking. She glanced at the men and Hal. They were watching her. She lost her voice. Motioning with

10

her hand for Levi to follow, she stood up.

As they disappeared behind the house, the men broke into a discussion about construction details on the room. In a few minutes, Levi and Emma came back. The two of them chatted comfortably as old friends tend to do.

John said, "Levi Yoder, what do you think of Emma's flock?"

"She has gute hens, Daed. Emma was not joking. She has a pet rooster. He will eat corn out of her hand, but his favorite food is flies. Emma has a quick hand. She is a gute fly catcher." Levi sounded impressed.

Luke teased, "When air is cool, flies are slow. Makes them easy to catch."

Emma's face turned beet red. Hal suspected that flush went clear to her toes.

"My daughter is gute at mothering birds and animals as well as all of us," John said proudly, handing Emma his empty glass.

Hal helped collect the other glasses so the men could get back to work. After she placed the glasses on the kitchen counter, she sat down at the table with Emma. For a while she folded her arms on the table and listened to the hammers while she wondered how to find out the answers to her wedding worries.

Emma broke the silence between them. "How about going outside with me to pick some dandelion greens for supper?"

"Isn't that a weed?"

Emma giggled. "Jah, but a very tasty one this time of year if you know how to fix it into a salad." She headed for the door.

"You'll have to show me what to pick," Hal told Emma.

They stepped outside into the bright light. Hal lifted her face toward the cloudless, pale blue sky and soaked in the combination of sun and a light, cool breeze.

Emma handed Hal a small knife. "Walk around the yard. You are looking for dandelion plants. They are slender, long, jagged-edged leaves. Later on, the plants will reach full growth and bloom a yellow flower. By then, the leaves are so bitter they not pretty gute." Emma bent over to slide her paring knife blade under a circle of flat leaves. She sliced a cut through the root at the ground's surface. Dropping the plant in her bucket, she said, "See. Just like that."

Hal was pretty sure she knew what to look for. She'd watched her dad put weed kill on dandelions in the yard often enough. Warm weather brought up other wild flowers, as well, in the Lapp yard. Here and there, wild violets peeked above the short sprigs of grass. Some were dark purple, some white and some white and lavender variegated.

With her back to Hal, Emma searched around her feet as she said, "You seem very quiet this afternoon. Is something wrong, Hallie?"

"I don't think so. It's just I had lunch today at the Java Alley Coffee House with my boss and friend, Barb Sloan. She asked me for information about the wedding. You know. A date and place. I couldn't tell her anything. Why hasn't your father brought the wedding up? You don't think he is changing his mind about marrying me, do you?"

"Stop!" Emma snapped.

Hal froze, wondering what she said that was so wrong.

• Chapter 2

Pointing at the ground, Emma said, "Do not step on that dandelion." She paused while Hal bent over to cut under the leaves.

As Hal dropped the plant in the bucket, she gave Emma a tentative look. "Well?"

Emma met that look. "No, that is not it."

"I have so many questions I need answered. I feel as if I'm being kept in the dark. I don't understand why John hasn't discussed what's going to happen next. I'm worried that he has decided I'll never fit in. Are you sure he's not changing his mind?" Hal asked matter of factly.

"Hallie, that is not it. You must never think that," Emma scolded. "He has not given the wedding much thought, because he knows there is a lot of time yet. Much has to be done before the wedding."

Hal wasn't so sure time was John's reason. How could Emma know for sure how her father felt. No matter what the reasons for delaying the wedding, she didn't like the sound of Emma's statement. "A lot of time? How much time?"

"Several months. Most weddings usually take place in November."

Hal gave Emma a sharp look. "November! Why so far

off?"

"Weddings are in November or December on Tuesday or Thursday. That is the choice of days to get married for couples that are marrying for the first time," Emma explained.

"I want to be a part of this family now. Aren't there any exceptions to the rule since your father has been married once before?" Hal asked in an exasperated tone.

"Do not get upset. Since my father has been married before, he will be allowed to remarry when he wants to. Everyone realizes a man with children needs a woman in the home. There is nah need to wait." She paused then added, "When the wedding will be depends on how soon you can learn our Deitche language and our customs. You must do that before you talk to our bishop. He will have the final say about you converting to Amish."

"Okay, I get it, but you don't have a church. Where will the wedding take place?"

Emma bent to cut a plant. "Usually at the bride's parents home."

"I don't have Amish parents."

Looking about her feet, Emma said calmly as if placating a child, "We will have the wedding here."

Forgetting about salad greens, Hal walked in front of the girl to get her attention, intent on finding answers to all her worries. "What about a wedding dress? Shouldn't I be shopping for that soon?"

"Jah. For the material so you can make it," Emma said with patience in her voice.

"This is terrible. I have to make the dress! I can't sew," Hal said, her frustration mounting. Emma giggled and hugged Hal. "We have a saying. Worry is like a rocking chair. It gives you something to do but does not get you anywhere. This wedding will be done like all Amish weddings, and it will happen. I can teach you how to sew. We can work on the dress together."

"But I don't know where to find white material," groaned Hal.

14

"Blue."

Sighing, Hal looked at the girl sideways as she asked slowly, "Blue what?"

"The wedding dress is always blue."

"Okay, I don't know where to find blue material or how much to buy."

Emma giggled.

Hal rolled her eyes skyward even though she realized the girl couldn't help it. Seeing Amish ways through Hal's befuddled eyes amused Emma. At the moment, Hal couldn't find any humor in this conversation. She had to try to look at life with the glass half full like she thought Amish people did. Maybe that would happen someday after she'd lived a long life with John. Hopefully by then, she would be used to Amish customs and beliefs. She could only hope she'd be able to look back and find this conversation as funny as Emma did now. "We need to go get the material soon. I don't care if all the formality seems a long way off to John. As slow a seamstress as I'll be, I need a lot of time. I don't even know where to start looking for blue material."

Emma patted Hal's arm, trying to sooth her ruffled nerves. "Bloomfield has a cloth store that stocks material for Plain customers. That is where I get the material for our clothes. I will be glad to help you pick what you need. Now we better finish picking leaves for the salad. Before you know it, it will be time to fix supper."

"Your father has asked me to go for a walk with him after supper," said Hal excitedly.

"Gute. Talk to Daed about the wedding," Emma said. "Mind coming with me to cut winter onions for the salad? The onion patch is by the field fence behind the chicken house."

"Onions come up on their own?"

"Jah, that is how they get the name winter onion. A green onion that dies down in the fall and comes up in early spring. Wild onions in the timber do in a pinch, but they are never as mild as winter onions. The blades are tiny. Takes time to clean them and more of them to cook with."

15

"You are so full of knowledge about such things. If I am to be a good cook, I need to know all that you know," Hal said sincerely.

"Teaching you to cook is not so important. I can do that task for the family. You have other things that are more important to learn right now. We need to start your Deitche lessons right away."

While Emma prepared the dandelion salad, Hal helped so she'd know how it was done. The girl placed six slices of bacon in an iron skillet near the front of the wood cookstove. Toward the back, she had a skillet of sliced potatoes and a skillet of pork chops frying. Another small pan held two eggs in boiling water. She popped the lid off a jar of green beans. As soon as she had the beans simmering, the bacon was done. Emma placed the strips on a plate to cool and poured the bacon grease in the green bean pot for seasoning.

She instructed Hal to wash and chop the dandelion leaves into small pieces. After that Hal chopped up the green onions and bacon to add to the bowl.

When Emma put ingredients for the dressing into the skillet she'd fried the bacon in, Hal said, "Tell me what you're putting in."

"First cream and butter. While the butter melts, I need to beat an egg in a bowl, add salt, pepper, vinegar, sugar and flour. When I have that all mixed together, I pour the egg mixture into the skillet and stir until the dressing thickens."

"That's it? You pour that over the salad."

Emma stirred the pot. "I like to let the dressing cool for a few moments so it does not wilt the dandelions too much. The last thing we do before we place the salad on the table is chop up the two boiled eggs into it. After that, we can add the dressing."

"I can't wait to try it."

After supper, John rose from the table. He looked directly at Hal. "Emma, think you can do the dishes alone? I want to go for a walk with Hal."

"Can we come?" Daniel shouted. His wide brown eyes

16

filled with excitement.

Serious-faced Noah, his dark eyes shining, slid out of his chair, ready to sprint for the door.

"Noah and you have homework to do," Emma reminded Daniel. "You should get at it."

The boys slumped back into their chairs. John ruffled Daniel's brown bowl cut hair, still concentrating on Hal. "Not this time, boys. I want to talk to Hal alone."

When they stepped off the porch, Hal shivered as the night air hit her. She paused long enough to pull her denim jacket closed and zip it. Gazing up at the maze of glittering stars, she thought about pinching herself to see if she was awake. She was that happy. She'd never imagine a time she'd feel like this. Not before she met John anyway. Now if only, she knew what was ahead of her so she could stop worrying about this new life she was about to start. Her concerns weren't newlywed worries about money, housing and getting along with the in-laws. She had to learn to speak Pennsylvania Dutch, figure out what was the best way to act around Plain people, what to expect from them and how to pass a bishop's test.

The large barn loomed out of the darkness, casting a moonlit shadow over them as they walked across the yard. Hal breathed in the fresh night air. "This is a lovely night."

John agreed, "Jah, it is that. We got plenty of light from that half moon."

"My father would say this is a night to track rabbits in the snow or hunt coon when it is this light out."

Sauntering along beside her, John looked off in the distance. "Is your daed a hunter?"

Hal hesitated. Should she answer truthfully about her father owning a gun and killing animals? "I'm afraid so."

"You need not worry about what I will think of your family. Parents that raised you have to be gute people," John complimented. "Besides I am sure your daed uses the animals he kills for food."

Hal smiled in relief. "Yes, he does." At least, John had it half right. They ate the rabbits. Now the coons were another

17

story, but she wasn't going to mention that unless John did first.

John held his hand out. "Give me your hand, Hal."

"I'm doing fine. This ground is so familiar to me I could walk this farm blindfolded," Hal assured him.

He stopped. "Hal, I just wanted to hold your hand."

With a girlish giggle, Hal said, "In that case, here it is."

As they walked along close together, John replied, "So you know my farm well enough you could walk it blindfolded." Hal heard humor in his voice.

She closed her eyes. "Of course, I can. Listen. Hear the sows grunting softly in their sleep." She leaned her head toward the pig pen. "On the other side and just behind us is the barn. I know because the horses are nickering. They hear our voices."

"Es a voonderball gute thing," John said, squeezing her hand.

"Listen to the peepers? That's a good sign that spring is here."

John paused to listen. "This is true if this is the third time."

Hal opened her eyes to look at him. "Third time?"

"When you hear the peepers twice and each time they are frozen back, the third time spring will be here to stay," John explained.

Hal studied John's profile in the moonlight. "I sure hope this is the third time. Where are we going?"

"Just over that rise in the hayfield so the three pair of eyes peeking out the window cannot see us in the dark," John said, chuckling.

"They wouldn't do that, would they?"

"Jah, they would," he assured her sincerely.

Once they made it to the end of the lane between the field and pasture, John turned loose of her hand. "We can sit down now."

Hal plopped down. She caught a whiff of the clover and alfalfa plants she crushed under her. John eased down beside

18

her.

"Listen now," he said softly.

"To what?"

"Silence. We are alone. Nah children after our attention," he whispered.

"Oh, but I like having your kids want my attention," Hal declared, scooting close to him so she could lay her head on his shoulder.

John put his arm around her. "So do I, but do you realize we never get to spend any time by ourselves?"

Hal looked up at him. "We should try to make time, shouldn't we?"

John put his hands on her face and kissed her gently. "Jah," he said in a husky voice. "I have been thinking. Finding time alone would be easier to come by if you move into my house."

"I couldn't do that," Hal stated tersely.

Taken back by her adamant reply, John asked, "Why not?"

"It's going to be hard enough to get the Amish community to accept me once we are married. It would be twice as hard and maybe not at all if I break a rule like living with you in sin. On top of that, my parents would see it the same way and be mad at us." Hal hoped she could make John understand. She was determined. She had waited this long to marry, and she wanted to do everything the right way.

"Looks like we would both have a problem. I do not want your parents upset with me and you any more than you want to be disliked by Plain people. We could say you are living in the spare bedroom so you will be close to the clinic," John suggested.

Hal was ready to change the subject. Since John brought up marriage, she decided this was the moment she had been waiting for to clear up a few things. "You have taken the time to give this a lot of thought I see. Have you given as much thought to our wedding? Because I've been wondering about it."

"What do you want to know?"

"Why we haven't talked about it? I've been afraid maybe you're having second thoughts about marrying me. Perhaps, you think the Amish people won't accept me, or that I'd never fit in. Maybe you want everything to stay as it is right now. In that case, there would be no need for a wedding," rushed out of Hal's mouth.

"Never think that. That is not so. You will fit in. You already do with my family," John said, giving her a light kiss. "You worry too much to yourself. Instead of keeping your thoughts in, you should talk to me about the things that worry you."

Hal tried to look into John's chocolate brown eyes but with his back to the moon, they were as dark as the night. "That's what Emma told me, but why do we have to wait? Emma tells me we can't get married for several months yet."

"That is so. You must use the time to let us teach you about the Amish ways. Bishop has to talk to you before he makes his decision. You need to be prepared if you are to convince him you are serious about being a part of my family and converting to our church community. I do not want to wait any longer than you do so move in with us now," he insisted softly.

"Do you know how hard that would be for the both of us with me sleeping in the spare room by myself and you in your bedroom?" Hal declared.

"I did not plan on you sleeping there," John whispered.

"Oh," she uttered. Hal gave that a moment's thought. "Oh, no, we can't do that, John."

"Why not?" Exasperation was clearly in his voice.

"For one thing, think of the children. What kind of an example does that set for them? They would be bound to catch on," she said firmly.

John ran his fingers through his shock of brown hair. "I guess you are right."

"We have sayings in my family, too," Hal said.

John asked dryly, "What is it?"

"Do you want to hear this one or not?"

"Jah."

"My father said when I started dating that I should tell the boys that there couldn't be any sampling of the milk before they bought the cow," Hal warned him.

John took a deep breath and conceded, "Your father was right to instruct his daughter that way. I will be sure to say the same thing to Emma one of these days."

"I took my father's advice to heart." She tried to look into John's soulful dark eyes. Hearing the woeful sound in his voice, she hoped that she was taking the right stance. "Believe me. For the first time in my life, I wish I wasn't still listening to my father's advice. I want so badly to be with you."

John tried to convince her again. "Move into the spare bedroom anyway and sleep there. At least, you would not have to make the trip into town every night. We can go from there. A step at a time."

"There is one other matter. What if we took one step too many, and I became pregnant? How would that look to the bishop?"

"What you are saying is true." John ran his fingers through his shock of hair. He was running out of arguments.

Hal shrugged her shoulders. "I guess I could get a prescription for birth control pills."

John's jaws dropped.

Hal said softly, "Not exactly the Amish way, is it?"

"Nah," He said quickly. Trying to be honest with her, he admitted, "I want to have children with you. Plain people have never disagreed with English taking birth control. We do not practice it, because we like large families."

"I want children too but only after we are married," Hal chided.

"That means we will just have to make do with waiting until after we marry whether we like it or not." He surveyed her with an intensity she wasn't sure she wanted to read.

"I guess so. When will I meet the bishop?" Hal asked.

"You already have."

21

"I – I have?" She sputtered.

"Jah, Eldon Bontrager is our bishop."

Hal's eyes widened. "Oh, my. That's one of the men that's helping build the clinic, isn't it?"

"Jah."

"But I like him. He seems like such a nice man."

John chuckled. "Jah. How did you expect our bishop to be?"

"I thought a bishop would be strict and serious. He'd be hard to convince that I want to be your wife and part of your way of life," Hal answered truthfully.

"Just because he is a gute friend, does not mean he does not take his duties as bishop serious even where I am concerned. He will be all of that you said and more when he talks to you about converting. He has to be sure you will fit in and mean to stay Amish. If he does not do his job the way he sees fit, he will have many Plain people unhappy with his decision to let you join. You have to prove yourself to the bishop and again to Plain people," John said seriously.

"I hoped my efforts to run the clinic would go a long way toward proving that I want to share this way of life with you and the Amish community," Hal fretted.

"Jah. That will help."

Hal put her hand over John's. "Don't you know I'd marry you tomorrow if you could arrange it?" Then she amended, "Well, maybe not quite that quick. We have to wait for my mom and dad to get here from Titonka in northern Iowa. Takes most of a day to drive here."

John withdrew his hand and shifted nervously on the ground.

"What is it, John Lapp? I can't ask my parents to my wedding?" Hal snapped.

"It just is not done. They are English. We never have English at weddings," he croaked, patting his beard.

"John, have you ever been to a wedding where an English woman married an Amish man?" Hal asked pointedly.

He had to admit, "Never have. It so rarely happens.

22

Plain people marry an English person after they leave the community."

"So if the bride is English and wants to be Amish, it stands to reason she could have a few English relatives and a few friends at her wedding. Don't you think?" Hal reasoned. "The groom has family and friends present, doesn't he?"

John groaned. "Jah, my two brothers and two sisters and their families and everyone from the community will be invited to ours." He gave a resigned sigh. "If this is what you want I will bring it up to the bishop." Hal perked up. John held up a hand to stop her from speaking. "Once he has agreed to your confirmation. It might be best not to bring this matter up right away. We must get through one thing at a time and take things as they come."

Chapter 3

In a matter of two weeks, the clinic was ready for use. When Hal arrived one afternoon, the men had only a small portion of roof left to shingle. John hurried down his ladder and escorted her into the clinic for a tour.

Emma waltzed in from the living room, eyes sparkling with excitement. "How does the clinic look to you, Hallie?"

"Wonderful," Hal said, giving Emma a hug.

The room smelled like new wood. The two windows southerly exposure gave the room light and warmth. John had built two cupboards and attached them to the wall to store medical supplies in. Two chairs and a small table had been placed in front of one window. A small bed, covered with a quilt of purple and blue squares, was along the back wall.

"I had the men stop long enough to set the furniture in so the clinic would be ready when you got home," John said proudly. "We just went back up to finish the roof."

"This is great. Now, all we need is patients," Hal said cheerfully.

Emma smiled faintly at her enthusiasm. "We should not wish bad luck on anyone by wishing to give them medical aid, Hallie."

"No. I didn't mean that. Oh, but, Emma, won't it be great for Plain people to have this clinic to come to instead of going all the way to Wickenburg."

"Worse yet, they might have suffered at home because they did not get help at all," said John, putting his arm around Hal's shoulders. "Now I should get back up on that roof and help the men." He gave her a light kiss.

Hal met Emma's twinkling eyes and blushed. As he went out the door, she said, "See you later, John."

Thundering of fast moving horse hooves dashed against road rock. Hal and Emma rushed outside. A small boy riding bareback on a work-horse galloped up the driveway.

When he spotted John in the yard, he pulled back on the horse reins. The excited horse threw his head high in the air. His nostrils flared as he sidestepped. The boy, his brown hair flying around his face, cried, "Help! Help!"

"Something is wrong with Jimmy Miller," Emma cried as she ran down the steps.

The pounding hammers ceased. The men slid to the edge of the roof and climbed down the ladder.

John rushed along side the horse and grabbed the reins. "Whoa. Whoa!" The horse came to an antsy stop, his sides heaving as he breathed. "What is it, Jimmy?"

"Mama sent me to get you quick. Daed's ladder broke. He fell down into the well. We need help getting him out," gasped Jimmy, his brown eyes filled with tears. The boy, about Noah's age, didn't wait for a reply. He kicked the horse in the sides and headed back the way he came.

"We will follow you," John yelled after Jimmy. "Elton, can we use your buggy?"

Hal grabbed John's arm. "That will take too long to get there. Let's use my car. My medical bag is in it. Just show me the way."

John looked from Elton to Luke and got their nod of silent approval.

As she ran to the car, Hal fished her cell phone out of her jean pocket and poked 911. Looking over the roof of the car, she hesitated long enough to ask John the Miller address. She got confirmation from the dispatcher that an ambulance

25

was on its way and opened her door. Elton, Luke and Levi got in the back seat. Emma and John got in up front.

The Miller farm was only half a mile away. Hal eased the car around Jimmy who was doing his best to stay on the slick back of the hard riding work-horse. The upset boy was sitting on daylight more than the horse's back, bouncing up and down with the heavy impact of each hoof.

When she drove far enough away from Jimmy, Hal sped up, raising a cloud of gray dust behind her. She hit a fairly deep pothole, bouncing her passengers off the seats.

"Sorry," she mumbled to no one in particular, keeping her eyes on the road to avoid as many other holes as she could.

The car shimmied for a time after hitting the pothole. The steering wheel vibrated under her fingers. She made a mental note that one of these days she had to leave the car at Earnie Long's to check the shocks. Maybe, the tires needed rotating. Earnie would figure it out if she ever found the time to stop at his car repair garage for more than a can of pop.

From a distance, Hal made out a windmill looming against the sky. Not far from it a large burr oak tree towered over the area. A woman and a small girl bent over the well opening in the windmill base. A neat set of white farm buildings sat just north of the well.

Hal slowed to turn into the driveway. The Miller mailbox post had a sign on it – Great peace they have that love the Lord. She past the barn and came to a stop by the windmill. Leaving the car doors open, the men and Emma bounded over to the well. Hal closed the doors and parked on the back side of the oak tree so her car would be out of the way of the ambulance.

She wasn't prepared for what she saw when she looked into the well. A wooden ladder floated on the water about twelve feet below. Pinned under the ladder, a motionless man bobbed, submerged face down. His straw hat clung to the casing, floating a slow circle around the well.

Hal glanced at the man's wife. Her first impression of Roseanna Miller was that she was a very pretty, young woman.

Knowing compliments didn't go over in the Amish community, Hal was sure Roseanna would never like being told that, especially not today. The woman's wispy, chestnut hair was neatly combed and tucked under her white head covering. Her light brown eyes focused on the well pit, wide in worry for her husband. Fear of what was happening to Emil Miller covered her long, slim face and filled her eyes.

The pale yellow-headed girl, with a splash of freckles and a turned up nose, clung to her mother's skirt. Silent tears streaked down her cheeks.

Taking charge, John turned to Miller's wife. "Roseanna, do you have another ladder?"

"Jah! In the shed." She pointed over her shoulder. She couldn't take her eyes off her husband.

Luke ran for the tool shed.

Hal edged over beside Roseanna. "Won't you and your little girl come with Emma and me? If we go over by the tree, we'll be out of the men's way."

Without looking at Hal, Roseanna nodded agreement, but she didn't move. Her little girl tugged at her skirt. Roseanna put her arm around her daughter's shoulders to comfort her, but she couldn't take her eyes off her husband submerged in the water.

Emma tugged on Roseanna's arm. "Please, come with us," she said softly.

As if Emma's words finally registered with her, the woman backed away from the well. Taking her daughter's hand, she moved the few weary steps it took to stand under the oak tree.

"Good job. She's listening to you," Hal whispered to Emma. Once they stopped by Roseanna, Hal introduced herself. "I'm Hal Lindstrom."

Leaning back against the tree so she could use it for support, Roseanna said in a drained voice, "I have heard of you. You are called Nurse Hal?"

Hal touched her arm. "Yes, that's me. How long has your husband been down in the well?"

27

"I do not know. Usually Emil tells me when he is going to replace the leathers, but this time he did not. Jimmy went looking for him and found his father like that." Roseanna stared at the well and a sob escaped. "He is so still under that ladder."

"Yes," Hal answered.

Emma put her arm around Roseanna's shoulders. The little girl crowded between her mother and Emma to be by her mother's side. "Hallie, meet Ella," Emma introduced.

Hal squatted and peered into the child's fear-filled, moist hazel eyes. "Hello, Ella. It is nice to meet you."

"I can't leave him," Roseanna cried wretchedly, wringing her hands. "I must go see if I can help."

Standing up, Hal stayed in front of Roseanna, making sure she had the woman's attention. "Emil has plenty of help. We need to stay out of the men's way."

"I need to do something. What can I do?" She asked desperately.

"Pray," Hal said firmly.

Roseanna looked Hal directly in the eye. A calmness came over her. She shut her eyes and bowed her head. Taking a cue from her mother, Ella did the same.

"Luke's coming with the ladder," Emma said softly.

Kicking up a trail of dust, Jimmy galloped over to the well and slid off the horse. The sweat lathered horse drooped his head, panting as he willingly stood still.

Luke leaned the ladder against the windmill. He handed Elton a rope and John some strands of wire. John wired the ladder to the well platform, sticking the shiny wires in the holes right next to rust covered, fragments of broken wires. He said in a low voice for only Luke and Elton's ears, "This was an accident that did not have to happen. Emil should have replaced these rusty wires long ago." He turned to Elton. "Once I get down the ladder toss one end of the rope down. I am going to slip it around Emil. Hook the other end to the horse's neck. When I tell you, pull back while I steady Emil on the way up."

As John disappeared from sight, Hal felt a streak of fear that he might suffer Emil's fate. She darted a glance at Mrs. Miller. It wouldn't do for her to show her emotions right then or to yell to John to be careful. What she vowed she intended to do later was to make John promise he would never go down in the Lapp well without telling someone. She never wanted to go through what Roseanna Miller had to deal with at that very moment.

In a few minutes, Hal heard John's voice, sounding hollow as it funneled back out of the well. "I'm ready. Start lifting."

Elton commanded the horse to back up as he walked alongside. The horse kept the rope taunt. Luke helped guide the rope from the well opening. Levi leaned over the platform waiting to help his father grab hold of Emil.

To Hal, the time it took to rescue the man seemed to go on forever. As she glanced at Roseanna, she knew that must be what his wife was thinking. Roseanna gripped her trembling hands together tightly, turning them white one second and rubbing them angry red the next.

The west wind blasts didn't help the anxious way Hal felt. For a space of time in the harsh quiet, all they heard was Elton's husky voice instructing the horse to back up. Then the silence was interrupted ever so often when a gust blasted the windmill's silver blades. The blades whirling motion increased wildly, creating a screeching grate of metal against metal. The sound set Hal's raw nerves on edge as she waited to go into action. How did the Millers or any other Amish family stand the noise of a working windmill day in and day out? Now that the thought came to her, Hal realized she had noticed the Lapp windmill before. She hadn't paid any attention to the sound. Besides, the windmill was the least of the things she had to get used to in the coming months. She'd ignore the noise once she became John Lapp's wife. Noises were just part of living on a farm.

Emil's bowed body appeared face up. He dangled limply, suspended from the rope wrapped around his waist.

Water rained from his clothes, splatting loudly as it flowed into the well. Emil's arms swung back and forth on their own. The man's long, drenched dark hair was plastered to his face. His head was thrown back on his arched neck. Luke and Levi reached for him and pulled the man away from the well opening and over the casing.

Water poured off Emil's dark blue shirt and black pants, making dark splotches in the dirt. Luke and Levi held him by the shoulders and Elton had his feet. Water made a trail of dark polka dots as they carried him to a patch of grass near the oak tree. The men gently laid him down.

Luke slid the rope along his body and off. He handed it to Elton to roll into a coil and unhook from the horse's neck. Pulling the reins over the horse's head, Elton handed the rope and reins to Jimmy. "The horse tie to the windmill for right now."

As Hal knelt beside Emil, Roseanna moved close behind her. "Oh Emil," she moaned. "Help him, Nurse Hal."

"I'll do what I can," Hal replied, leaning over to put her ear on his chest. Not even a faint heartbeat could be heard over the water gurgling in his chest.

Emil's mouth gaped open. His lips were blue. His skin was a ghostly white. Water seeped from his nose and ears. She checked in his mouth to see if she needed to clear it. Visible water had already dripped out while the men carried him. Putting her hand under his neck, she pushed the man's head back. Placing one hand over his forehead to hold his head in that position, she pinched Emil's nose and blew as hard as she could into his mouth to move air through the water in his lungs.

She kept that up for what seemed like an hour, but in reality was probably only minutes. Finally, the screaming ambulance pulled into the driveway. It made a U turn in the open field, back up to the group and stopped. The ambulance's double doors burst open. Two men hopped down and pulled the gurney out of the back. The driver, a woman, slid from the cab and raced over. She knelt beside Hal.

Without looking up, Hal stopped long enough to say,

"I'm Hal Lindstrom, RN with the Wickenburg Home Health Department."

The woman placed a finger on the side of Emil's neck and pressed in, checking for a pulse. "When did you start CPR?"

Hal blew in his mouth, then raised her head to the woman. The fast movement made her head fuzzy. "Maybe ten minutes ago."

The men lowered the gurney beside Emil.

"You must be ready for a rest. Let me take over," the woman said.

Hal rose and backed up. John and Luke helped the two men slide Emil onto the gurney in one swift movement. The woman bent over Emil and continued CPR as the men rolled the gurney to the ambulance. She stopped long enough for the EMTs to fold up the wheels and hoist the gurney into the back. The woman hopped in beside him. As the doors shut, Hal could see her leaning over Emil again.

"Mrs. Miller, the ambulance is taking your husband to Wickenburg Hospital," Hal said.

"I must go there," Roseanna said urgently to the air in front of her. She took a halting step, heard a cow bawl and froze. "The cows ----. It will be time to milk before I get back. Emil would never be late for milking. I have to hitch up the buggy. I must hurry." Her mind jumbled with an overload of thoughts.

John took charge again. He put his hand on Roseanna's shoulder. "Hal can take you and the children to Wickenburg in her car. That would be quicker. If you do not mind riding in Nurse Hal's car?"

The pale-faced woman looked from Hal to her car. "I want to be with my husband."

"Gute," John said, "You go with Hal. If these men are agreeable, they can help me with the milking. Do not worry about chores." He turned to Hal. "The boys will be home from school by now. Stop and tell them they will have to milk alone tonight."

"All right," Hal said. "Mrs. Miller, come around and get in the front with me." She took Roseanna by the elbow and lead her around the car. The woman moved along only when prompted. Hal opened the door. She waited for Roseanna to get in the car. The woman started to sit down then turned to Hal. "My husband is in a bad way, ain't?"

"Yes, it doesn't look good, but the ambulance crew will be doing CPR on him all the way to the hospital. A doctor in the emergency room has been alerted that Mr. Miller is on his way. Everyone is doing all they can for your husband," Hal assured her.

"I am glad to hear that. Thank you for all you did to help Emil," Roseanna said, patting Hal's arm. Then she ducked her head and sat down.

Emma slid in back with Jimmy and Ella. As Hal drove past the mailbox, she read the sign again. She hoped Mrs. Miller took the saying to heart. Roseanna was going to need to pray for peace in her heart in the coming days.

In a few minutes, Hal pulled into the Lapp driveway. "Emma, find the boys as quick as you can." Emma slid from the car. As an after-thought, Hal got out, too. She said softly, "Emma, I think it would be good if you came to the hospital with us. The Millers will need a friend they know. Mr. Miller's condition isn't good."

"Jah, I understand. I will hurry," Emma said over her shoulder, darting to the house.

Hal drove into the hospital parking lot just as the ambulance pulled away from the wide portico. The automatic doors opened to let Hal, Emma and the Miller family troop into the ER. The fluorescent lights stark brightness bounced off the white walls and shiny, waxed tiles underfoot. Used to the dim light of kerosene lamps and candles, the Amish children wilted. They lowered their heads and focused on what was in front of them. As nurses and doctors in green rushed around them, the children looked both fearful and curious about this unknown world.

"Where do we go?" Roseanna's worried face focused

32

on the line of cubicles down the hall, wondering which one her husband was in.

Hal stopped them at the nurse's station and leaned over the counter to speak to the nurse. "Hi, Lucy."

The nurse stood up from her paperwork. The petite woman's head just barely showed above the nurse station counter. She smiled when she recognized Hal. "Hi, Hal. The Amish man that just came in yours?" She asked briskly.

"Yes. This is the Miller family. Roseanna Miller, this is Lucy Stineford. We worked together at the Home Health Department until she got this ER job," Hal introduced.

"Why don't all of you go sit in the waiting area. Doctor Christensen is with your husband Mrs. Miller. I'll tell him where you're at," the nurse said gravely and rushed for a cubicle with the door closed.

The television, in the waiting area, was on. The evening news with Charlie Gibson was playing. Hal always liked the way Charlie presented the news. He blended the worst events with human interest stories surely designed to make the viewers feel better about all the bad news he gave them.

Hal studied Roseanna. The poor woman didn't care about terrorists or falling stock markets right now. All she wanted was to hear good news about her husband. She clutched her hands at her waist, trying to hold herself together. She stared at the closed exam room door as if she was willing her husband to walk out of that room to her.

Ella and Jimmy's eyes widened in fearful awe as they stared at the pictures flickering on the television. The phone trilled loudly at the nurse's station. Ella jumped. Too many English inventions to cope with while the children worried about their father. Hal picked up the remote on the lamp table and did away with Charlie Gibson.

Doctor Stan Christensen's voice brought her around. "Hello, Hal." Standing in the doorway, the tall, blonde, blue-eyed man, dressed in green scrubs, with a stethoscope around his neck, had a harried look on his face.

Lucy stood behind him. Hal darted a questioning glance

33

at the nurse. Lucy gave a slight nod of her head. Hal caught Emma's eyes and nodded toward Roseanna. They both moved close to her.

Hal said the doctor, "Dr. Christensen, this is Roseanna Miller."

He turned to Roseanna and offered his hand. "How do you do."

"My husband?" Roseanna whispered, gripping the doctor's hand.

His was the sad face of a man who no matter how many times he delivered bad news couldn't get used to it. "I hate to tell you this, but there wasn't anything we could do for your husband. Mr. Miller was in the water too long. He was gone before he arrived at the hospital."

Roseanna covered her face and sobbed. Jimmy and Ella put their arms around her as much for their own comfort as to comfort her.

"Nurse Stineford needs to get some information from you. After that you can go home," the doctor said gently.

The nurse held up a clipboard she'd kept by her side. "I'm sorry for your loss, Mrs. Miller. I need to ask which funeral home to call."

Roseanna took a deep breath. "Schrock's."

Briskly, the nurse said, "Thought that might be the case since they have the horse-drawn hearse. If you will sign a release form for the funeral home, we will take care of the rest." She handed the clipboard to Roseanna.

"May I see my husband for a moment?" Roseanna asked as she handed the board back.

Lucy nodded. "Of course, you can. For as long as you want. Follow me."

Roseanna took a step. She weaved back and forth unsteadily. Hal grabbed her and put an arm around her shoulders. "Do you want me ----," Hal hesitated when Roseanna gave her a blank look and continued, "Emma to go with you?"

Taking a deep breath, Roseanna stiffened her back.

34

"Nah, we will not be long. Come kids."

Supper at the Lapp farm was late that evening. Absentmindedly, Hal nibbled at her fried potatoes and scrambled eggs as she watched the children focus on their full plates. The boys were friends with Jimmy Miller. Having lost their mother, they related to the loss Jimmy and his sister were going through.

As long as Hal had known him, Noah, twelve, had too serious a demeanor for a child. Now his solemn expression said he was grieving for the Millers. He kept his dark eyes on his plate as he pushed potatoes slices around in a pretense at eating.

With a gloomy face, Daniel, ten, rested his elbow on the table and leaned his head on his hand. He had taken a bite of egg but he chewed it forever while he tried to digest the loss Jimmy and Ella had just faced. Both boys had many of the features of their father, but Daniel's soft brown, wide doe eyes were the path to his heart and soul. Right now, the boy was traveling a sad journey within himself.

Pale-faced and weary, Emma must be reliving in her head the scenes of Emil's rescue. Tough moments for a young girl to have to witness. However if she intended to give medical aid to her community, moments like this afternoon would be what made her strong enough to handle a crisis.

Hal hated that the Lapp children had to struggle with a loss so soon after putting the loss of their mother to rest. Coming to grips with that had taken them almost two years, but then that was their mother. After she understood why the children held on to mourning Diane Lapp, she helped them push that aside. They had become alive again. If she needed to, she would just have to help them through this.

Hal thought about her mother. What advice would she give these children for this situation? Experiencing death was part of growing up. Loving and losing relatives and friends is part of living. That should work. Probably, Amish think the same way. Then again, Hal didn't think her mother was used to facing the types of accidental deaths that occurred on an Amish farm. I'm pretty sure since I've been living in Wickenburg I haven't heard of an English farmer that drowned in his well.

While helping Emma with the dishes, Hal asked, "Do you think the boys will have a hard time dealing with Emil Miller's death.

"It will bother them for a while. Mostly worry they do about Jimmy and Ella," Emma said.

"I could see that just looking at them at supper. They hardly ate anything," Hal worried.

"The death of our mother was hard on all of us. The circumstances of Emil Miller's death bring back our mother's passing, but we are taught gelassenheit. That is a help," Emma said thoughtfully.

"Gelassenheit? What does the word mean?"

"Our lifestyle. We are raised to live life with serenity, quietness of character and submissiveness to God, church and family. Add gelassenheit to hard work and you have the Amish way of life. Think you can live like that, Hallie?"

"I love your father and you kids so I certainly intend to try," Hal said with conviction.

"Put your worries aside. After the funeral is over, our lives will go on in the routine they always do," Emma predicted.

Hal asked, "When will the funeral be?"

"Day after tomorrow. Men are building a pine box to set the coffin in already. The funeral home will bring Emil home. Some of the men will dress him in a white suit. After that, Plain people will gather to pay their respects. The minister will speak for about three hours. All the buggies get a chalked number on the side so people can line up to follow the hearse to the cemetery. The minister leads a spoken song, and everyone says the Lord's Prayer over the grave. After the funeral is over, everyone meets back at Roseanna's farm and has a light lunch."

"I should find someone to replace me tomorrow morning at work so I can come," said Hal.

"Nah," Emma said shortly.

"Why not?"

Emma shook her head. She watched the steam from the soapy dishwater fog up the window as she said, "Nah outsiders are allowed to come to a funeral."

"Oh," Hal uttered, chastened by Emma's tone.

"This is the way we do things. That is why English call us Peculiar people. Our ways are different," explained Emma.

Hal winced. "It's just that I keep forgetting I'm an outsider."

Emma's eyes softened as she put a plate in the rinse pan. "I did not mean to hurt your feelings. The time will come when you can go to funerals with us."

Hal smiled wryly. "I know. You've said it before. Patience is a virtue."

"Jah," said Emma and went back to washing dishes.

A couple mornings later, Hal stepped out of Wickenburg's Senior Citizen apartments. She watched a robin hop across the dewy lawn, looking for a nightcrawler. A gentle breeze rustled newly leafed out tree branches and fluttered her curls. The robin egg blue, cloudless sky was cluttered with a crisscross of narrow, smoky jet trails.

The slow, rhythmic click-clack of horse hooves made Hal look down at the end of the block. It was as if she had walked into a time machine and flew back a hundred years. She stared at two sleek, black horses slowly pulling a black wooden hearse past the apartments. Dressed in a black suit, the driver, a somber expression on his face, focused straight ahead. Through the large window in the hearse's side, the pine casket was in easy view. Schrock Funeral Home was taking Emil home.

Chapter 4

"Gute afternoon, Hallie. Tea water is ready." Emma said, rolling her sleeves up. "Make us both a cup. I will be done with the bread soon."

That suited Hal. She was good at tea making. It was the first cooking lesson Emma gave her. In no time, she had two cups of tea ready and sat down to watch Emma knead the bread.

The girl sprinkled a hand full of flour in a circle on the table. She dumped the pale lump of dough out on top the white spot. Placing the dough between her floured hands, she leaned on it, stretched it and flattened it. Quickly, she pulled the dough toward her, shoved at it and balled the dough in her hands. Pushing the lump back across the table, she started over. After a repeat of movements, she rolled the dough into a ball and threw a dish towel over it.

Emma washed her hands and sat down. "Now in about an hour, I will repeat what I did. Once the dough is in loaf pans, we leave it to raise again for an hour. Then the bread is ready to bake," Emma told her and took a drink of tea.

Hal blew on the steaming cup in front of her and took a sip. "I saw the hearse leaving town this morning. Was there a lot of people at the funeral?"

"Jah, Plain people turn out gute to pay respects."

38

"How is Roseanna holding up?"

"She is in mourning. Living without Emil will take some getting used to," Emma predicted.

Patches let out a long series of barks. Hal pulled the curtain back and looked out the window. Heading for the clinic, she said over her shoulder, "We have a patient."

A young boy limped up the porch steps, favoring his right foot. They met the boy at the door. Emma took him by the arm and supported him until they reached a chair. "Welcome, David Leichenring to our clinic. Come sit down."

"Hi, I'm Nurse Hal. How old are you, David?" Hal pulled the chair out for him.

"Eight," he said, giving her a once-over with his bright blue eyes.

"What did you do to your poor foot?" Hal asked.

"I stepped on a rusty nail," he said, scrunching up his face in pain.

"Are you going barefoot already?" She couldn't help the surprise in her voice, but she knew she had hit a touchy subject with David. The boy turned red and ducked his head to hide his face under his straw hat. He managed a nod

"It's too cool to be without shoes. You are rushing things," teased Hal.

"Jah, des is what Mama said," he answered meekly.

"You don't want to hear it again, do you?" Hal pulled the other chair around in front of the boy. "Put your foot up on this chair so I can see the bottom."

The bloody, mud-caked hole was just below the dusty toes. Hal opened a cupboard door. She took out the supplies she needed and lined them up on the table.

"Emma, go get me a pan of warm, soapy water, a washcloth and towel. I need to wash David's foot." As Emma hurried from the room, Hal said to the boy, "This will sting."

"Gute afternoon, Hallie. Tea water is ready." Emma said, rolling her sleeves up. "Make us both a cup. I will be done with the bread soon."

That suited Hal. She was good at tea making. It was the

first cooking lesson Emma gave her. In no time, she had two cups of tea ready and sat down to watch Emma knead the bread.

The girl sprinkled a hand full of flour in a circle on the table. She dumped the pale lump of dough out on top the white spot. Placing the dough between her floured hands, she leaned on it, stretched it and flattened it. Quickly, she pulled the dough toward her, shoved at it and balled the dough in her hands. Pushing the lump back across the table, she started over. After a repeat of movements, she rolled the dough into a ball and threw a dish towel over it.

Emma washed her hands and sat down. "Now in about an hour, I will repeat what I did. Once the dough is in loaf pans, we leave it to raise again for an hour. Then the bread is ready to bake," Emma told her and took a drink of tea.

Hal blew on the steaming cup in front of her and took a sip. "I saw the hearse leaving town this morning. Was there a lot of people at the funeral?"

"Jah, Plain people turn out gute to pay respects."

"How is Roseanna holding up?"

"She is in mourning. Living without Emil will take some getting used to," Emma predicted.

Patches let out a long series of barks. Hal pulled the curtain back and looked out the window. Heading for the clinic, she said over her shoulder, "We have a patient."

A young boy limped up the porch steps, favoring his right foot. They met the boy at the door. Emma took him by the arm and supported him until they reached a chair. "Welcome, David Leichenring to our clinic. Come sit down."

"Hi, I'm Nurse Hal. How old are you, David?" Hal pulled the chair out for him.

"Eight," he said, giving her a once-over with his bright blue eyes.

"What did you do to your poor foot?" Hal asked.

"I stepped on a rusty nail," he said, scrunching up his face in pain.

"Are you going barefoot already?" She couldn't help

40

the surprise in her voice, but she knew she had hit a touchy subject with David. The boy turned red and ducked his head to hide his face under his straw hat. He managed a nod

"It's too cool to be without shoes. You are rushing things," teased Hal.

"Jah, des is what Mama said," he answered meekly.

"You don't want to hear it again, do you?" Hal pulled the other chair around in front of the boy. "Put your foot up on this chair so I can see the bottom."

The bloody, mud-caked hole was just below the dusty toes. Hal opened a cupboard door. She took out the supplies she needed and lined them up on the table.

"Emma, go get me a pan of warm, soapy water, a washcloth and towel. I need to wash David's foot." As Emma hurried from the room, Hal said to the boy, "This will sting."

Emma was such a homebody. It pleased Hal to watch the girl's head turn one way then the other like a bobble-head doll, trying not to miss the scenery they flew by. "How does sightseeing in a car compare to a buggy?"

"Our buggy may take longer, but it is much easier to take everything in," stated Emma.

Hal couldn't argue with that statement.

Emma looked at her sideways. "Sometime when Daed is not using the buggy, I will give you the experience of going on a toot the Plain way."

"Can't wait," Hal said dryly. "What is a toot?"

"What we are doing today. Going shopping. Sooner or later, you will have to get used to riding in a buggy," Emma said seriously. "It is the way you will be traveling."

Looking straight ahead, Hal tried to digest the feeling of loss she had over the prospect of losing her car. How was she ever going to get used to a slower paced life? She liked getting from place to place as fast as she could. Fudge! I love my car. She took a deep breath and decided to put aside this worry until she had to face it. This trip was meant to be a happy time for Emma and her. She wanted to keep it that way.

Emma giggled as she watched Hal's face. "Not having

your car will not be like losing your best friend. We can hire Elsa Mast, a Mennonite neighbor, to drive her car for us. For a few dollars, she will take us anywhere we need to go."

"That's good to know," Hal conceded halfheartedly. Soon they arrived in downtown Bloomfield. Hal drove around the town square. "Where's the fabric shop?"

Emma watched as they turned a corner and pointed middle ways of the block. "Right there?"

Hal pulled into a parking place in front of the fabric shop that had a large sign above the door that said Sewing Center. All stores around the square were reminiscent of those Hal was used to seeing in Wickenburg or Titonka. Side walls joined walls. Tall, stone buildings had large signs above the doorways. On each side of the signs, molded white arches adorned the long, narrow windows.

Each store had the same view, a stately courthouse in a park-like setting in the middle of the square. Hal glanced up at the clock tower. In defense of her car, she wondered if she should mention driving to town gave them more time to shop before they had to get back to bake bread. Maybe not. That was her problem most of the time. She just couldn't let touchy subjects be. Well, there was always later on the ride home. She just might bring up the need for speed in her car if Emma worried about her loaves of bread rising over the sides of the pans.

Emma shaded her eyes with her hand and turned in a circle, studying the store buildings. "These buildings are so tall, they make me dizzy just looking up at them."

"Oh, Emma. The height of the buildings are nothing compared to buildings in large cities," Hal declared.

It had been years since Hal had been inside a fabric shop with her mother in Titonka. Along the walls, shelves were stacked high with bolts. Tables scattered about the room were filled with folded stacks.

The sight of all that material gave Hal an overwhelmed feeling. "Where do we start looking?" She asked in amazement. Now she knew how Emma felt when she looked at the tall buildings.

Emma grinned. "Follow me."

The girl took off across the room and through a doorway. Didn't take long for Hal to see why that room held Emma's interest. The tables were filled with material used for clothing needs of the Amish.

Emma said, "Here we can find material for anything we need."

They circled the tables full of polyester bolts while Emma searched for what she wanted. Bolts of dark colors – plum, cranberry and navy blue covered some tables. Other tables held soft pastel shaded material - greens, lavenders, pinks and blues. One table held only black cotton for slacks, dresses and bonnets. Another one was filled with bolts of sturdy black wool and denim for coats and jackets.

Emma turned to Hal. "There are many choices of blue. You pick."

"I think I like the light blue. Would that be all right?"

Emma picked up the bolt. "It is a pretty color. Now pick out three more colors for dresses. One to wear shopping and visiting and two for every day. You need black material, too. You will have to wear a black dress occasionally," Emma instructed. "I'll take a black bolt and a white one to the counter while you pick the others. The saleswoman can get started cutting."

"I thought you said I didn't need white," Hal said.

"Not for the dress but for the cape that fits over the dress top and the apron," Emma told her.

Trying to be practical, Hal chose plum and navy blue material for every day. She picked a soft green for a dress to wear shopping and visiting. Once Emma found spools of thread to match each material selection from row upon row into a spool display, Hal laid out the cash on the counter. The clerk stuffed all the material into two large bags.

As they carried the bags to the car, Emma said gleefully, "I can not wait to get started."

"Yeah, me, too," said Hal halfheartedly.

Inwardly, she was groaning. She had to bite her tongue to keep from complaining. Talk about Amish folks seeing the glass half full. That was just what Emma did. She looked at the various material sticking out of the bags and saw a whole new wardrobe for Hal. Dresses that would make her look Amish. All Hal saw was hours of pinning pattern pieces and cutting material. After that came the multitude of stitches it would take to make her look Amish. She went in that store for enough material to make a wedding dress. Just one dress, not five. Emma had done it to her again. Seemed like every time Hal let that girl help her, Emma took over. Give her an inch and she took a mile. The only half full thought she could muster was she'd surely be able to sew by the time they finished five dresses.

Hal glanced again at the courthouse clock. "That didn't take long. We have plenty of time left. Why don't we do some shopping while we're here? For something besides dress material, I mean," Hal suggested.

"I could use to go to the drugstore once," Emma said.

Hal pushed the cart while they wandered up and down the aisles at Rexall. Emma put deodorant and hand lotion in the cart. Hal picked up a box of gauze to replenish what she had used in the clinic.

"I think that will do it for me," Emma said.

"Do you suppose there's a gute place to eat around here?"

"You did not fress dinner?" Emma gave her a disapproving look.

"I did so," Hal shot back. "I thought we might have a piece of pie. I can always eat dessert."

Smiling, Emma led Hal across the intersection onto the next block. On the corner was Mom's Kitchen, a cafe where farmers and town folk alike headed first thing each the morning. They discussed gossip and anything to do with farming over a cup of coffee. By noon, they were back for a plate of home-styled cooking.

Hal and Emma sat down in wooden chairs at a chrome-legged table with a yellow top. A young waitress, not much older than Emma, came toward them. Her ponytail swayed back and forth as she hurried. Her white tennis shoes had silver lightning bolts running along the sides. The lighting caught the bolts, sending glinting flashes across the floor.

Watching her come, Emma, with disdain, looked the waitress up and down.

"What can I get you?" The waitress stopped smacking her gum long enough to ask. She poised her book in midair.

"We're going to have pie with a scoop of vanilla ice cream on top," Hal said. She read the handwritten list of pies on the menu board behind the counter. "I want boysenberry."

The waitress shifted on her feet to look at Emma.

"Apple." Emma watched the waitress leave, giving her head a slight shake of disapproval.

"Her's is a whole other life," Hal defended.

To sum it up, Emma said cryptically, "English life."

Supper time came and went without John at the head of the table. The children didn't seem to mind nor notice. Hal did. After supper, the boys spread their homework out on the table by the living room window. Emma rushed to do the kitchen cleanup. Trying to help, Hal picked up the butter bowl. Emma snatched it from her and headed for the cool room. She came back in time to grab the salt and pepper shakers out of Hal's hands and set them in the cupboard. At a whirlwind speed, the girl came back at Hal again. Hal froze not knowing which way to go. Emma darted around her.

The girl grabbed the teakettle off the cookstove and poured steaming water into the dishpan. She plopped in the stack of plates. A wave of hot, soapy water splashed over the side of the pan. Sudsy foam cascaded down the counter front. Emma grimaced at the mess she'd made as she took one quick swipe at the wet cupboard door. She straightened up and rubbed a plate with such speed, Hal was having trouble keeping up with the girl's hands. Before Hal had time to dry that plate, Emma had all of the others washed, plus the silverware and cups. While she waited to fill the rinse pan with stainless steel pots, Emma washed the table and counter. In a flash, she dipped the last pot into the rinse water. She dried her hands on the hand towel above the wash-pan and threw the dishwater out the back door.

"Done," she said, wiping out the aluminum pan.

Folding the wet dish towel over the towel holder at the end of the counter, Hal said, "I feel like I just ran a marathon. What is your hurry?"

"What is a marathon?"

"A long, tiring foot race. You ran the race, but I'm worn out just watching," Hal joked.

"We need to get busy," rushed from Emma's mouth.

"Why?"

"I want to put the wedding dress material on the table. If we get the cutting done tonight, we can sew in the evenings," Emma explained.

"Do we have to keep the dress where your father can't see it?"

Emma said slowly, "I can not think of a reason why we would."

"Uh, well, English brides think it's bad luck to let the groom see their wedding dress," Hal explained.

Emma giggled. "That is one worry Plain brides do not have. The groom already knows what the dress looks like. All wedding dresses are alike."

"I see. How will we know how big to make the pieces? We don't have a dress pattern."

"We do. Wait here." Emma flashed out of the room. She came back carrying the material. On top were pieces of yellowed newspaper. "The pattern is cut out of newspaper. It was a pattern my mother used for her dresses. You are about the same size so I am sure it will fit. Let me hold the pieces up to you to see for sure."

Emma held each piece of the blouse against Hal. She gave Hal a pleased smile. Hal assumed that meant the pattern pieces suited the girl. "Now stand still. I'm going to hold the skirt piece against you so we get the length right." Emma held up several pages of newspaper penned together in a row. "Hold this to your waist. I need to place a straight pen where I must cut the material middle ways of your lower leg. Mama must have been taller than you."

While Emma knelt on the floor, Hal did as she was asked. She would feel much better about going to all the trouble to make this wedding dress if John was home. She kept wondering what he was doing. It seemed awfully late for him to be away. Maybe he had trouble milking Roseanna's cows, and it took him longer. Noah and Daniel didn't take that long to milk. They finished hours ago. She knew she should stop worrying. When John came home, he'd explain.

Hal had to concede Emma was right as usual. They should get started on the dress. Knowing how Emma thought, she wondered if the girl was doing her best to keep Hal occupied while they waited for John.

Emma spread the material out on the table and handed Hal a pin cushion.

"What's this for?" Hal asked.

"I will lay the pattern pieces on the material. You pen them down."

Hal did as she was instructed. After she wove the last straight pen in, she backed away from the table. "That's done. Now don't expect me to cut on that material. I'm a nervous wreck just thinking about it."

"I can cut, but you watch so you know how it is done," Emma said with her I mean it voice. Making a stack of cut pieces and one of folded scraps, she handed two scraps to Hal to keep them separate. "We will give your attendants each a scrap. They must buy the same material for their dresses so they match yours."

Another thing Hal hadn't thought about. "How many attendants?"

"Two."

"They have to be Amish?" Hal asked, knowing what the answer would be.

"Jah."

47

"Will you be one, Emma?"

The girl gave her a quick hug. "I would be honored. Who will be the other?"

"I'll have to think about it," Hal said. "It's not like I have a bunch of Amish friends to pick from."

"Trust me. You will. Everyone will love you, Hallie, once they know you," Emma assured her.

Hal twisted her head to listen outside. She hoped John would be home before now. He wasn't, and she was tired. Wickenburg seemed a long ways off right then. "Emma, it's time I went back to town. I won't want to get up in the morning for work," said Hal with a yawn.

Chapter 5

The black and white milk cows grazed in the pasture. John's large, temperamental bull trod in a patrol along his pen fence, making a trench in the dust. He searched for a way to get to the cows. A black and red rooster flew up on the pig pen fence. He crowed several times loudly as if he was announcing Hal's arrival. Like anyone at the Lapp farm cared that she had shown up. No sign of John anywhere. Patches didn't even jump out of the ditch to greet her. The best she could hope for was to find Emma in the kitchen. That was always a given.

Holding a bowl cradled tightly in her arm, Emma vigorously stirred chocolate cake batter.

Hal peered in the bowl. Quick before Emma could protest, Hal stuck her finger in the batter to get a sample. "That for supper?"

"Jah," Emma said, concentrating on beating the lumpy mixture.

"Yum." Hal sniffed. She inhaled again, deeper this time. "Why doesn't the house smell like food today?"

"I did not cook. Daed is far behind with fieldwork. Emil Miller's funeral took half a day. Now he gets a late start and stops early to do Roseanna's chores." Emma busied herself, pouring the batter into a greased cake pan. She popped the pan in the oven and wiped the counter off to get rid of brown drops of cake batter. "It worries me that Daed did not eat. He should not go hungry while he is working so hard."

"You are right about that," Hal agreed.

Emma had a suspicious glint in her eyes when she turned around. The kind of look that made Hal leery if she took the time to think about it. "If I give you a lunch for Daed, would you take it to him?"

"Sure. He should stop long enough to eat."

"You will find him in the west field." Emma pointed west out the back door and handed Hal a dishtowel bundle.

Hal tromped in long strides over the large chunks of slick, gleaming black dirt in the freshly plowed field. She had to be careful not to fall down and keep a tight grip on John's lunch at the same time. It occurred to her, sneaky Emma had set her up again but in a good way this time. Emma could have taken her father his lunch at noon, but she knew how lonesome Hal had been lately. The girl purposely waited for her to show up.

Hal kept her eyes open for John staggering across the field behind a plow and team of draft horses. Over the next rise, she heard the pop-pop of a tractor motor before she could see it, growing louder as it came nearer. Hal's mouth dropped open when she topped the rise. John was coming in her direction on a 50's vintage white tractor with steel wheels. He had his head twisted over his shoulder, watching the three bottom plow dig in and flip the clods over.

How about that. John Lapp owned a tractor. Old for sure and no rubber tires but not at all the picture she had of him struggling along behind a team of work-horses. Hal looked behind her and across the unplowed ground in front of her. John was almost done. The hay field fence was not far away.

"John! John!" Hal waved frantically to get his attention.

At the sound of her voice, Patches jumped out of the fence row grass and came loping to meet her. John searched around him. When he spotted her, he waved back with a big grin and stopped the tractor. While he waited for Hal, he jumped down and picked up a handful of dirt. John smelled of it. Hal was reminded of how often she had seen her father do the same thing.

"Patches, you deserted me to go to the field with John," Hal joked as she patted his head. "Come on. I have to deliver lunch."

John climbed back onto the tractor. He called, "Come here once. What are you doing out here?"

Hal ran to him, holding the dish towel bundle up for him to see. "Emma said I was to get you to stop long enough to eat lunch. She doesn't want you to go hungry, and neither do I."

She handed John the sack. He laid it on his lap. Holding his hand out, he helped her up on the tractor and gave her a kiss. "Have a seat on the fender. We can talk while I eat."

Left without Hal's attention, Patches took off down the fence line, sniffing for a rabbit.

"Why didn't you stop to eat?" Hal asked, easing onto the slick fender. The metal, heated by the sun, felt good as the warmth soaked through her jeans. She took the dish towel from him, put the bundle in her lap and untied it.

"I lose all track of time when I am working." He gave her a boyish grin as he set the quart jar of hot coffee beside his feet. Picking up the peanut butter and jam sandwich, he started to take a bite, changed his mind and said, "Reminds me of a story about a farmer that had a large family. The man had been chopping wood all morning. His wife hollered at him to come eat lunch. He laid the ax down, but he tripped over it and fell down. He got right back up and went back to chopping wood. Later when his wife asked him why he did not come in for lunch, he said he wasted so much time falling over the ax he figured there would not be any food left to eat." He took a bite of the sandwich.

Hal giggled. "That excuse might work if there had been a lot of people sitting at your table during lunch, but Emma was alone."

The warm breeze fingered through Hal's curls. She swiped the wayward hair out of her eyes so she could look out across the field. This was John's life, wholesome with fresh air, farming the earth and raising animals. The same way of life her parents chose. The life she had when she was growing up.

Patches barked an excited woof when he spooked a rabbit. The gray blur of fur streaked off down the fence row with the dog jumping up and down in last year's tall dried grass after it. John turned his ear to the wind and listened. The wail of a train whistle broke the silence, like a song carried on the breeze for miles and miles. Here was a man that was tuned in to every country sound and sign. Hal loved that about him.

She surveyed the remainder of the field left unplowed. "Won't be long until this field will be done."

"This job, yes. Dragging the field and planting the corn is next." He looked up at the western horizon. "I hope the weather holds until I get done. Once the spring rains start, they pretty much do not know when to quit." He finished the sugar cookie. After he took the last drink out of the coffee jar, he placed it back in the middle of the dish towel. While Hal knotted the towel, he gave her a solemn look.

Thinking that was the end of this conversation, she made a move to rise. Without a word, John held his arms out to pull her close. She was more than willing to go to him. He rested his cheek in her springy curls. "I have missed you."

Hal looked up at him. "That's nice to hear. I miss you, too."

He put her head in his hands and kissed her. Smiling, he said, "That kiss was worth stopping for, but now I need to get back to work."

"I know," Hal said and climbed down off the tractor.

Without saying much that night, Emma and Hal did the routine kitchen clean up as swiftly as they could. Once while washing the dishes, Emma stuck one soapy finger against the white curtain that covered the bottom half of the window. She pulled it back for a quick look toward the barn. She let the curtain drop back into place and scrubbed rigorously on a pot.

Hal knew what Emma was thinking. The girl wished her father would hurry up and get home. She wanted Hal to be happier than she was. Hal had the same wish, but along with wishing John home came other worries stampeding through her mind. What was he doing at Roseanna Miller's farm at that very moment? Why did he spend so much time at the Miller house?

Emma brought the light blue dress pieces to the kitchen. As she dropped them on the table, the newspaper patterns rattled. She pulled the end of the thread out of the slit on the spool and stuck it in her mouth to wet it. Holding a needle with the eye toward the gas lamp, Emma threaded it and handed the needle across the table to Hal.

"Oh, you will need this," she said, bringing a thimble out of her apron pocket.

"This isn't yours, is it? I wouldn't want to take your thimble. You'll need it," Hal predicted, thinking about how much sewing the girl was going to have to do for her.

"Nah, it is my mother's."

"Oh." Hal reached slowly for the thimble, feeling a twinge at using something that belonged to Diane.

Emma sensed her reluctance. "I am sorry. We should have thought to pick one out for you when we bought the fabric and thread. Next time we go to the fabric store, I will remember."

"I don't mind. This will do for now," Hal told her, trying to sound like she meant it. The last thing she wanted to do was make Emma feel bad when the girl was so willing to help her.

While they sewed, Emma helped Hal learn Pennsylvania Dutch words by saying a word and giving its meaning. Hal repeated the word until she pronounced it right to suit Emma before they moved on to another word.

Concentrating on one of the blouse's shoulder seam, Hal breathed a sigh of relief when she made the last stitch. She knotted the thread, reached for the scissors and snipped. "Now I've got that seam done. How does it look?" Hal laid the pieces down in front of Emma for inspection.

The girl's shoulders drooped.

53

"What's wrong?" Hal asked.

"If it was basting we wanted, the seam would be all right, but the stitches need to be a lot smaller."

Hal grabbed the blouse back and stared at her work. "Are you sure this won't do?"

Emma arched an eyebrow at her. "Do you want your wedding dress to fall apart during the wedding?"

"No!"

"You can sew over those stitches. Make very small ones next time," Emma said, going back to work on a skirt seam. "Now what was the word for horse?" Hal didn't answer. Emma looked up and asked, "Horse?" Hal concentrated on her stitches. It was clear to Emma that Hal's mind wasn't on the lessons. Emma patted the table to get Hal's attention. "What is bothering you? Are you worried about the seam? I can sew it for you if you want me to. Do not worry. I will not let you wear a wedding dress that will fall apart at the wedding."

Hal laid the blouse down. "That's not it. My heart just isn't in sewing tonight. I keep thinking about your father. I miss him.

John is never home anymore in the evening. We had such a brief moment together this afternoon. Why does it always take so long for him to do chores at the Miller farm?"

"Roseanna has almost as many cows to milk as we do," Emma replied, not looking up from her stitches.

"Why aren't any of the other Amish farmers helping Roseanna out? Isn't that what they are supposed to do?" Hal complained.

"With spring fieldwork, they are all busy. They will take turns one of these days," Emma assured her.

"Doesn't it seem like it takes John a long time to get done with the Miller chores? Noah and Daniel have been done for hours now, and John still isn't home," Hal persisted.

"After he gets the milking done, he is staying with Roseanna until after supper," informed Emma, keeping her eyes on her sewing.

"Why?" Hal asked sharply.

Emma put her attention on Hal. She said evenly, "She feels as if she can repay him in some small way for helping her if she feeds him a meal. Daed feels she needs some company for a while. She is having a hard time getting over her husband's death."

"I see." Hal had the feeling she'd just been reprimanded for not having compassion for Roseanna Miller and her family. The face of the pretty, young widow flashed into her mind and stuck there, smiling at her. She didn't want to sound like she was complaining with such sad circumstances heaped upon Roseanna Miller. That would make her look like a heartless, uncaring person, but she needed and wanted John Lapp's company, too.

"Daed will be home this Sunday during the day between doing Roseanna's chores. This is our in between Sunday. No church. You can spend the whole day with him, ain't so?"

At last, Emma had said something that pleased her. "All right! I can hardly wait," Hal said and went back to concentrating on her stitches.

Chapter 6

That May Sunday, the temperature was in the middle 60's with a slight breeze. Mid-morning, Hal eagerly rushed out to the Lapp farm. John's horse and buggy were sitting by the barn. He was home. She was so busy looking for John she didn't spot Patches in time to slow down. He sprinted out of the ditch and raced at her front car tire. She braked hard and fishtailed in the loose gravel, narrowly missing him. Hal's heart thudded in her chest as she fought to get straight in the road. By the time she stopped, her car leaned on the edge of the ditch. Hands shaking and stomach flip flopping with nausea, Hal put the car in motion and turned into the drive.

The ping of gravel flying and screech of brakes brought John rushing from the barn. Weak-kneed, Hal slid out and slammed the car door. Shaking from head to toe, she leaned against the car, holding her head in her trembling hands.

John trotted to her. "Are you all right?"

"Yes. Just a little unnerved. Patches ran at my car again. I was so happy to see you were home, I wasn't thinking about him. He took me by surprise." She paused, gave John a tearful look and predicted, "One of these days I won't be able to stop fast enough."

"I'm sorry this happened to you," John said, pulling her to him.

She felt his strained breathing from running. She wondered if he was able to hear her pounding heart. "Ever since I hit that deer, the thought of hitting another animal and winding up in the ditch unnerves me. I certainly don't want to hurt Patches."

He patted her back as he looked over her shoulder at the happy go lucky dog trotting toward the barn. "Patches is all right. By the way, I am so glad you are here."

Hal looked up at him. "Oh, so am I." It was tears of joy that moistened her eyes this time.

"We should enjoy today. Recht?" John asked, running a finger along her cheek.

Hal nodded at him.

With her hands on her hips, Emma stared down at them from the porch. "What happened? Are you all right, Hallie?"

Noah and Daniel peeked out the open door as Hal licked her lips and tried to sound normal. "Good morning, Emma. I'm fine. Patches just gave me a scare. Can I help you get dinner?"

"If you would like," Emma said, motioning toward the door.

John gave her a peck on the cheek. "I have to finish up in the barn. I will be in shortly."

Noah and Daniel sat back down at the table and resumed a game of Scrabble. As Emma headed past them, she said, "Brothers, go out and two fryers catch. We will have fried chicken for dinner."

The boys frowned. They eyed each other and looked at Emma with a do we have to look. They didn't want to stop their game.

Hoping to give them a reason to do as Emma told them so they wouldn't get in trouble, Hal said, "Can I help? It has been a long time since I butchered chickens with my mother. I'd like to help you."

Smiling at her eagerness for such a mundane task, Noah said, "Come with us."

"We will give you a treat," snorted Daniel.

57

Emma turned the chickens loose early each morning. Luckily, a few of the fryers had gathered back in the hen house. They were still young enough to be uncertain about the vast world outside their safe place. Noah took the catcher, a stiff wire with a hook on one end, off the wall. Daniel motioned for Hal to step inside. He closed the door. Spying humans, the mixture of hens and roosters crowded under the roost in a tight cluster. Noah slipped up slowly so he wouldn't spook them. He eased the hook around the leg of a dark red and black rooster. With the precision of experience at this chicken catching job, he jerked back. The rooster protested with a loud squawk, flogging the floor with his wings. Hal could see by the window's light the rooster stirred up particles of sunbathed dust that floated in the air. She wrinkled her nose at the stifling odor of ammonia. Small, fluffy feathers fogged up from the floor, fanned into flight by the rooster's wings.

"You are a very good rooster catcher," Hal complimented.

Noah nodded as he carried the rooster upside down by the legs and handed it to Daniel. Again he eased the catcher under the roost. The chickens were on the alert this time. They crowded each other for a spot within the center where they thought they would be safer. With the slightest touch of the cold wire hook, the chickens moved their feet up and down to avoid getting caught. Noah inched the hook into the cluster and snagged a hen's leg. As he drew her out of the flock, she cackled an alarm to the rest. Noah jerked the hook forward so she could step out of it. Suddenly, a nice fryer tromped his way to the outside of the flock. Noah saw his chance, hooked the rooster and pulled the protesting squawker out from under the roost. He handed the chicken to Hal.

"Now you have to take the roosters behind the chicken house," Noah said to Hal. "There is a block of wood back there. I need to get the hatchet from the tool shed to cut their heads off."

After they stepped out into bright sunlight and fresh air, Daniel said, "Come on, Nurse Hal." He sprinted for the back of the building.

As Noah disappeared toward the tool shed, Hal's nose began to burn. She sneezed, getting rid of what chicken dust she'd inhaled. That sneeze might have been what scared the rooster into action, but Hal figured him to be a noisy fighter anyway. She held her catch at arm's length to keep the rooster from flogging her with his flapping wings. He emitted a squawky, threatening growl and suddenly doubled his body up like a contortionist. Rearing his head back, the rooster pecked Hal's hand. Surprised, she squealed and dropped the rooster. A spot of bright red blood oozed from under the broken skin at the base of her thumb. With a triumphant squawk, the rooster took off low and fast across the yard. The last Hal saw of him, he disappeared around the house.

Fudge! No way was she going to catch up to that chicken. What was she going to do? She hated to tell the boys that she wasn't able to do something as simple as hang onto a rooster after she invited herself along to help. They would be sure to tease her. Besides she let part of dinner get away. Now Noah had to catch another chicken. Emma would be waiting on them, expecting to get those fryers in the skillet soon. Noah and Daniel might think she was too much bother to let her ever help again. The last thing she wanted to do was make the boys think she couldn't do such a simple job.

A loud, long crow came from behind her. She turned just as a rooster flew up and perched on the corner fence post near the chicken house. Maybe she could catch him before the boys spotted she was empty-handed. She edged toward the rooster with her hand out.

"Nice rooster," she said softly. "Stand still."

Cocking his head sideways, the rooster kept his black beady eyes on her, watching her slowly move in his direction.

Dancing nervously from one bright yellow foot to the other, he flapped his wings, ready to take flight.

Hal stopped. "Don't leave," she pleaded softly, still holding her hand in midair.

The rooster flew off the post, but instead of running

59

away, he landed on the ground a few feet from her.

"Nice rooster. Don't move. Nice rooster," Hal cooed.

With proud strutting steps, the rooster actually moved slowly toward her. What luck. He must think she was going to feed him. Maybe he liked the sound of her voice. Who knows what a chicken was thinking. She certainly didn't nor at this point did she care. She had to catch him before Noah came back, or Daniel peeked around the chicken house to see what was keeping her. She squatted down, still holding her hand out.

"Come to me, rooster. Please come to me," Hal said softly.

The rooster strutted sideways with one wing dragging on the ground. He danced in a circle just out of her reach. Suddenly, Hal remembered how she had been chased and flogged by her mother's mean roosters when she was a kid. She noted the long spurs protruding on the back of this rooster's legs. She decided to slowly stand up. No way did she want that rooster to attack her face. A spur dig at her jean covered legs wouldn't hurt nearly as much.

The rooster pranced toward her. He was so close now. She could almost touch him. Hal took one quick, long step and grabbed. Her fingers clamped around the rooster's long, curved, black and red tail feathers. She pulled the squawking bird off the ground just as Daniel called, "Nurse Hal, what's keeping you?"

Throwing a handful of long, arching tail feathers on the ground, Hal replied, "Just slow, Daniel. I'm coming." She was proud of herself. She had caught a rooster by herself without the boys helping her. Too bad she couldn't brag about it, but at least now they need never know she lost the other one.

After lunch, as Hal put a handful of silverware away, she asked, "Emma, what are we going to plant in the garden?"

"This family likes many different vegetables," Emma said. She opened a drawer and took out a worn, frayed notebook. She handed it to Hal.

"What is this?"

"Turn to the last page that is written on. You will see

60

where I have drawn lines for rows. Beside each row is the vegetable or flower's name we will plant this spring."

Hal opened the book on the table. The two of them leaned over it as Emma pointed out rows labeled peas, beans, beets, carrots, turnips, potatoes, lettuce and more. Around the edges, she planned to plant orange cosmos and yellow marigolds. The very back row nearest the house, Emma saved for her tall green cannas that bloomed a red flower. She had a basket of dried bulbs stored in the basement.

"I didn't realize a garden took so much planning," Hal said, mystified by the thought Emma had put into her garden.

"It is important to rotate the crops so I do not grow a vegetable in the same spot too long. If I keep track each year, I know that will not happen," Emma told her.

Hal heard the restless shift of feet. She looked up to find John leaning against the doorway with his hands in his pants pockets. He had been listening to them. The smile on his face and the beam in his eyes told Hal he was proud of his daughter's friendship with the woman he planned to marry.

He said, "Are you two about done planting garden in here?"

"Jah, for recht now. We are going to continue for real soon enough." Emma said, putting her notebook back in the drawer.

"Gute. Hal, how about going for a buggy ride with me? We should enjoy this gute afternoon," he invited.

"I'd love to go for a ride," she exclaimed, giving him a hug. When she rode with him during the winter, she'd just had the car accident with the deer. She was hurting all over and had a concussion. That day, she wasn't about to enjoy anything, especially the jarring buggy ride.

"Gute, I did not leave the buggy hitched to the horse for nothing," John said, keeping an arm around her shoulders as he headed her for the buggy.

Everything about the countryside was springing to life. Hal enjoyed being outside in the fresh air. Best of all she liked spending this rare leisure time alone with John. As they headed down the road away from John's farm, Hal asked, "I've never been this way before. Where are we going?"

"No where in particular. I just like to see how far along my neighbors are coming with their spring work."

Me too, thought Hal. Maybe if John can find one of the farmers about done, I can suggest he ask about getting help with the Miller chores. "Spring is such a relief after winter, isn't it? The grass is greening up. Trees are leafing out." Hal took a deep breath. "Smell. The air is so fresh."

"The air is cool. Are you warm enough?"

"Yes, I'm fine," she said, laying her head on his shoulder. "How soon do you start to plant corn?"

"I am about ready. I plant corn when the leaves on the oak trees are the size of a squirrel's ear," he told her. "We are passing Elton's farm." John nodded off toward her side.

The large, two-story house in a neat yard with a garden by the road, a chicken house, a tool shed, an outhouse, a large barn and a windmill nearby reminded her of every other Amish farm. As Hal studied her feet, she reflected on the thought that in the Amish look-alike list of clothes and horses she could add farms.

She was about to reply that the Bontragers had a nice farm when a hunkered down mouse streaked over the toes of her tennis shoes. Hal screamed. She didn't think it was a big scream, just a long, shrill eek. Not that the type of her outcry made a difference to the horse. His ears swiveled back like radar, trying to detect where the danger was located. The startled horse's head flew up. He stretched his long neck out and bolted.

John sawed the lines back and forth. He yelled repeatedly, "Whoa, Ben."

Hal braced herself against the back of the seat. With one hand, she held onto the seat. With the other, she covered her mouth so she wouldn't repeat the same mistake again. The enclosed buggy must have hit every pothole in the horse's path. Hal had to take her hand from her mouth and place it on top her head to cushion the blows when she connected with the buggy

62

top.

Moving fast by blurred farmland and buildings, Hal wondered what Emma would think of the view on this ride. A quick glance at John's clamped jaws, with a twitter of tension in his cheeks, told Hal he wouldn't think her comment funny. The thought struck her that if the horse didn't turn the buggy over and dump her out, once John got the horse stopped, he just might do it himself. She edged to the end of the seat and braced herself in the corner.

The horse slowed down. He was tired out and breathing hard. John kept up the see-sawing on the lines. Ben was paying attention now. Finally, he stopped.

"Gute. We will sit here a minute. Give the horse a breather." John said, looking irritated. He cocked an eye at Hal. "Why did you scream like that? Have you never been around horses?"

Hal said in a tiny voice, "No, not really. But, John, a mouse scared me when it ran over my feet."

"A mouse." John gave her a nonplus grimace. That wasn't a gute enough excuse for her scaring the horse.

That look was enough for Hal to find her voice. "Didn't you see it? An icky, nasty creature. You know how I hate mice. Oh, John, I'm sorry. Right this very minute that mouse is under your side of the seat. Can you please catch him before he comes back over here by me?" She stopped when she realized she was babbling.

With a twitch at the corner of his mouth, John said, "I will try. Not for you but for the horse's sake. He will not want to go for a hard run again today. Here." He handed Hal the lines.

She stared at her hands wrapped around the leather lines. "What --- What am I suppose to do with these?"

"Drive while I look for the mouse," he said as if he saw nothing wrong with that idea.

"How?" Hal gasped.

"I will help you get started." John took the lines from her and shook them over the horse's back. "Get up, Ben."

The horse started off at a slow walk.

"Oh, I think this is a bad idea," Hal warned him.

John handed the lines back. "Ben is too tired to be much trouble. Just do not scream again and change his mind."

"Oh, I won't," Hal vowed, staring at the plodding horse. "Not as long as I'm driving but hurry and catch the mouse."

As he sank to his knees, John said over his shoulder, "Just hold the lines. Let the horse do the driving."

Hal had no intention of doing any different since she hadn't had any training for this. She sure hoped the horse knew what to do on his own. She put one of the lines in each hand. Unconsciously, she drew the left line tighter than the right line as she watched her feet, worried she'd see a streak of gray again. Worse yet. What if that awful creature ran up her pant leg. She'd just have to bail out and leave the driving to Ben for sure. She would depants in the middle of the road and hope no one came by.

John's back moved up and down as he stretched his arm under the seat. He groaned and grunted as he squeezed into the small space. Hal prayed the mouse stayed on John's side. She glanced at the gravel road to see where they were. It was a four-way intersection with farm fields on all sides. The horse decided to make an about face. He trodded docilely back toward home. If that was what Ben wanted to do, it was all right with her. She wasn't about to mention the horse turned around to John. She wanted him to concentrate on catching that mouse.

They passed an Amish man in an enclosed buggy as he pulled up at the stop sign. He waved at her. She nodded back. Since her hands were full, she couldn't wave. She hoped he didn't consider her unfriendly. Searching the floor around her feet, she inquired, "How are you coming, John?"

"He is a quick one. I keep missing him," came the stoic reply.

"Oh, no," groaned Hal softly so as not to scare the horse.

She looked through the buggy's front opening. The horse made another turn in the middle of the road, heading back the way they had been. Ben pulled the buggy past the other intersection. At that stop sign, a farmer, in a blue and white GMC pickup, gave her a one finger farmer wave. She acknowledged by nodding at him before the horse turned and crossed the road again. Now they were passing the Amish man and headed back toward home. The man was laughing so hard his straw hat slid off his head and disappeared from sight. Hal looked out around the enclosed buggy. For the life of her, she didn't know what he found so funny. She saw nothing to laugh at. If that man had a mouse in his buggy, he wouldn't be such a happy fellow.

Ben turned the buggy again and headed passed the pickup. The farmer pushed his cap bill up with a finger. He bent his head toward one shoulder and gave her a nonplussed look. What was his problem? Maybe he thought it strange to see an English woman, with bushy, red-gold hair, driving an enclosed buggy.

The horse plodded along slowly, following the narrow groove of buggy tracks he'd made in the road. Hal was getting tired of Ben's choice of routes when he made another turn and headed back past the pickup. Enough with the circles. For Pete Sakes, why can't this horse go straight?

John, in action, rocked back and forth on his knees. He swiped faster with his hand under the seat. The silence was broken by a series of squeaks.

Hal watched her feet as she asked through clenched teeth, "John, what's happening down there?"

"I got him," he cried.

"Thank goodness." She relaxed back against the seat.

Pleased with his catch, John pulled himself up and sat back on the seat. The mouse dangled, trapped by his back legs between John's two fingers. He continued his nonstop squealing. John held the mouse toward Hal so she could see the creature to prove he caught it. As if she couldn't hear the protesting, nasty, little varmint.

65

They passed the farmer in the pickup. Forgetting about the mouse, John took in what was happening. His attention was on the horse's turning again for the umpteenth time. John's mouth fell open. They rolled by the enclosed buggy parked at the stop sign. The flushed Amish man had his head cocked back against the seat, laughing hard enough that he held his stomach.

"That is Samuel Nisley," John said in a surly tone, waving at the Amish man.

Eying the mouse which was now too close for comfort, Hal decided she had her own problems. The critter pawed the air with its tiny feet, trying to reach Hal. She sputtered, "K- k - keep that creature away from me."

At the sound of Hal's voice, John focused on her. He said flatly, "We are going in a circle."

"Oh, that. Yes," she answered meekly, looking out the window.

"How many circles have we made?" He asked.

Hal wrinkled her nose at him. "I – I lost count."

"Why are we going in a circle?"

"You said let Ben do the driving. That was the horse's choice," she said, shrugging her shoulders.

"From the looks of the tracks, he has been circling for some time. Hal, you did not notice we are holding up traffic?"

"I know it. Now make the horse stop it." She thrust the lines at John.

John grinned. "All recht. Here you hold the mouse while I drive."

"You are joking! I hope. I don't want that thing. I will not hold him," Hal said indignantly, hiding her hands under her armpits.

With a glint in his eyes, John said, "All recht, you make the enclosed buggy go straight then."

"How?" They were passing the farmer's pickup. He had his neck stretched out and resting on the steering wheel. His nose looked inches away from the windshield as he stared at them.

John shook his finger at Hal's hands. "See how you are holding the lines. The left one is pulled tight. That makes the horse's head turn. Where he looks is where he's signaled to go. Loosen that line up to match the right one. The horse will quit turning."

Hal's lips flattened together as she did as he said. Fudge! She knew somehow this would all turn out to be her fault. The horse followed the wheel grooves down the road. Instead of turning, this time he headed for home. Hal just couldn't keep her attention on the road. Watching the mouse double up just like the rooster did before she let it get away, Hal asked, "I suppose it was my fault we went in a circle. I tried to tell you letting me drive was a bad idea."

"Jah, but I should have given you lessons before I asked you to drive. I did not think about you not knowing how," John admitted.

"I'm so sorry, but you are right. Emma never lets me cook anything without showing me how first." She felt absolutely hopeless. No wonder that man in the buggy had a laughing fit, and the farmer looked so bumfuzzeled.

"Do not worry. I can teach you what to do."

"John?"

"Jah?"

"Could you get rid of that awful mouse and take over. I think I've had enough driving practice for one day. I'm pretty sure Ben has had enough of me," declared Hal.

John chuckled as he threw the mouse out his window. He took the lines from her. The rest of the way home, Hal listened attentively as he gave her driving pointers. The lesson didn't end there. Once John backed the buggy into the lean-to, he showed her how to unhitch Ben and lead the horse to the pen.

"Think you got all that?" He asked as they walked to the house.

"Maybe but I wouldn't want to hitch up and drive anytime soon by myself," Hal assured him.

Emma met them at the door. "Have a gute ride?"

Hal said without enthusiasm, "It was fine." She held her breath, waiting for John to spill to Emma her horrible driving experience.

All he said was, "Jah, a gute ride."

Emma's eyes narrowed as she looked from her subdued father to Hal. "How are the neighbors coming with their field work?"

"Never noticed." John headed for his rocker. "I think I'll read my bible awhile."

Avoiding Emma's scrutiny, Hal wondered if John had to find a bible passage that would help him bolster his courage to take her as his wife.

"It is time to gather eggs," Emma said.

"I used to help my mother," Hal stated. She realized she had said that phrase a lot lately as if that qualified her for any job. Hadn't helped her so far. She failed most of the simple everyday chores.

Picking up the egg bucket in the mudroom, Emma said, "Come along. I want you to meet my pet rooster, Zacchaeus."

Following Emma, Hal asked, "Why did you name a rooster, Zacchaeus?"

"Because he always has to be up high to survey his surroundings and check on his flock. I named him after Zacchaeus in the bible. He was a short man who climbed a sycamore tree in order to see Jesus, because people in the crowd was so tall he couldn't see over them," Emma told her. "Here, Zacchaeus," she called.

Not one of the roosters and hens that showed up seemed friendly. Cautiously, they stalked around at a safe distance, checking the ground to see if Emma scattered corn. The girl looked through the flock. She stepped inside the hen house. "That is strange. He is not here. He usually comes when I call. Maybe he is still out by the barn. After I gather the eggs, we can look there."

Emma toted her filled bucket carefully as they walked by a wooden coop beside the chicken house. A long, burst of clucking came from inside.

"What is going on in there?" Hal wanted to know.

"That is a setting hen. She must of hatched. Hear her talking to her babies?" Emma opened the door. She hunkered down and looked in. "I see a little yellow head sticking out from under her wing."

"That is good," Hal said.

"Ach! Ach, nah. It cannot be," Emma moaned.

"It isn't good?" Hal asked bewildered.

Emma clutched her apron in her hands and gave Hal the most disconcerting look. "We can let the hen out so you can see for yourself. She might as well go to the chicken house tonight. Stand back."

"Didn't the hen have a good hatch?"

"When the hen and chicks come out, you will see for yourself. Help me count to see how gute her hatch was," said Emma, sarcastically.

The hen slinked to the door and peeked out. She looked back at her babies, clucking all the while. When she saw Hal and Emma, she bristled up, warning them to stand back, before she stepped into the grass. Twisting around she called her chicks to come to her. The chicks darted out and zoomed under her. The hen wasn't about to stay that close to the coop now that she had her freedom. She walked off the chicks, clucking to them to follow her and keep up. Peeping in protest, they scrambled along on shaky, newborn legs.

Pointing her finger at each to keep track, Hal counted seven chicks covered with reddish fuzz mingled with yellow. The top of their head had a dark brown stripe that ran down their backs. They reminded Hal of baby quail. Four others were larger, covered in downy, yellow fuzz. They had large, orange web feet and flat, wide, yellow bills.

Emma stared at the brood, shaking her head in disbelief.

Hal said, "I count eleven." She pointed at one of the yellow babies. "Why are some of the chicks so much different looking from the others?"

"They are not chickens. They are ducks," Emma said

69

tersely.

"That can't be. A chicken can't have baby ducks. It's not possible," Hal protested.

"Ach, it is very possible, if duck eggs were put under my hen."

"Did you do that?"

"Nah, but I am going to ask my brothers if they know who did?" Emma responded brusquely. She hustled to the house, set the egg basket on the table and headed out the front door to the barn. Still in his rocker, John looked up in surprise as Emma flashed by. He gave Hal a questioning look, but she just shrugged her shoulders. How would she know what had the girl so upset? Her intention was to trail along behind and find out. This afternoon had been bad enough for her. Now it didn't seem to be going well for Emma.

The only consultation Hal had was whatever was wrong with Emma wasn't her fault. "Emma, what's so wrong with hatching ducks?"

The girl turned around. "They are bigger and stronger than my chicks. The ducks will crowd out the chicks when they need the mother's warmth. If the chicks survive that, the baby ducks will steal all the little chicks food because they grow so fast. Grown ducks are nasty. They will murk up the chicken's water. The yard will be full of nasty piles of poop."

The screen door banged shut. John came down the steps with his hands in his pockets. "How do you know the boys are guilty of such mischief?"

"The ducks are wild mallards. Easy to find eggs in nests around the pond," said Emma hotly.

As he stepped around Emma, John mumbled, "I had lost track of time, reading my bible. The generator is going. The boys started milking already. I need to help." He opened the barn door and stepped in.

Looking one way than the other in the barnyard, Emma called, "Here Zacchaeus."

No rooster in sight. Not even a hen. The flock had gathered around the chicken house, ready to roost.

"He's not here, either. I'll ask my brothers if they have seen him." Emma waited for her father to clear the barn door. She stepped inside. "Have either of you seen my pet rooster today?"

Staying put outside seemed like a safe idea to Hal. She peeked past Emma. Noah was letting in a round of cows. Daniel was behind the stanchions, putting feed in the troughs. The boys yelled a loud no in unison, raising their voices over the generator motor.

Emma snapped, "You both say nah so easily. Now answer this question for me. Do you know anything about my brood hen hatching ducklings?"

His eyes intense, John leaned on a scoop shovel handle, watching his children. Noah looked at Daniel. They shrugged their shoulders and gave their father an innocent look. Noah bent down to attach the milking cups to a cow. Daniel flew by Emma and opened the feed room door to get a bucket of pig feed. He rushed back by his sister to feed the cows.

"My sons should own up to a practical joke," said John evenly.

Daniel's scoop stopped on the way to the feed bucket.

Noah rose up, placed his hand on the bony flank of the cow and turned to his father. "Jah, we put the duck eggs under the hen. Emma, I am sorry we did that."

John prompted, "Daniel, do you have something to say?"

Daniel emptied the scoop into a trough. "Jah, Daed. Emma, I am sorry we upset you."

"All right. I should be fixing supper. You, my brothers need to finish your chores. We can finish this subject later." She turned to Hal. "One of these days, I will show you Zacchaeus after I figure out where my brothers have him hid."

71

Chapter 7

The sun glowed a narrow beam of light through the clinic window, making a shiny spot on the table. Sitting in its warmth made Hal sleepy. She yawned and tried to keep her heavy eyelids open. Monday was always a draggy day, but this one was the draggiest. She had tossed and turned all night, barely getting to sleep before the alarm went off. By the time she dragged herself out of bed, she feared she was going to be late for work. She almost wouldn't have cared if it wasn't a worry to her clients. Mrs. Johnson would be on the phone to Barb Sloan if she was more than five minutes late. She lucked out and made it to Mrs. Johnson's apartment with thirty seconds to spare. Even with that much leeway, the woman had her hand on the phone, ready to dial Barb when Hal stuck her head in the door and announced herself.

Patches sauntered past the window on his way to the shade of the maple tree. This afternoon, she pulled in the Lapp driveway before Patches made it out of the ditch to chase her. He must have dozed off. She wondered if he'd had a bad night, too. He did his customary three circles and laid down to finish the nap she'd interrupted. Toward the back of the clinic, blue and purple clothes, white underwear and two of John's black pants snapped back and forth in the gusty breeze. Scratching in the grass under the clothes, the setting hen clucked to her baby chicks and ducks. By the fence behind the clothes, a large lilac bush was covered with purple flowers. The yard smelled with nature's sweet air freshener.

Holding a handful of garden seed packets, Emma interrupted Hal's revelry. "If you are not busy, want to help me plant some garden?"

"Sure. Looks like no one needs my nursing help this afternoon." Maybe the fresh air will revive me, she thought.

"That is gute," Emma said.

Hal opened the door and followed Emma out on the porch. "Where is the garden?"

Emma nodded toward the road. "That bare spot."

"I wondered why there wasn't any grass there, but I kept forgetting to ask. Why did you put milk jugs in the garden?"

"There is a danger of frost until in the middle of May. The jugs protect the cabbage and tomato plants I set out," Emma explained.

Hal didn't remember seeing vegetable sets in front of the feed store or at the tree nursery. "You bought sets somewhere this early?"

"Nah, I raised them from seeds."

"Why do you have the garden alongside the road?"

Hal could tell that sounded like a silly question to Emma. "Why not?"

"No reason. It's just that my mom had her garden back behind the tool shed. It was sort of out of sight," Hal told her.

"Why would I want to hide my garden?" Emma seemed perplexed by the idea. She dropped the seed packets at the end of the garden. "It is of interest for Plain people to see how their neighbors gardens are doing when they drive by. Even English like to see what kinds of vegetables and flowers are planted in them."

Changing the subject, Hal said, "Nothing better to eat than fresh vegetables from the garden."

Emma nodded agreement as she went down on her knees. "We have to raise enough to can for winter. You want to learn how to preserve food?"

"Yes, I do. If you think you can stand trying to teach someone who is as dumb as I am about such things," Hal said sincerely.

"Oh, Hallie. You are not dumb. Now we are going to start by planting radishes, lettuce and peas," Emma said, sorting the seed packets. A distant rumble turned her attention to the western sky. "Looks like a rain is coming. Dark clouds are banking up. If we hurry maybe we will have some of the planting and my chores done before the storm. I have been trying to start chores early so I can look for Zacchaeus."

She handed Hal the seeds before she picked up a hoe she dropped in the grass earlier. Giving the mellow dirt a whack with the hoe, she walked backward, making a small trench.

"What do you think happened to him?" Hal asked. Opening a packet of radishes, she bent over and dropped the seeds in the furrow.

"If he decided to roost out, a coon, skunk or possum could have got him. Maybe even a coyote. But he never does that," Emma declared. "I think my brothers had something to do with his disappearing. It is a joke on me."

"I can't believe that Noah and Daniel would do that to you," Hal said, opening the package of lettuce. She followed Emma as the girl made another row.

"Remember the duck eggs under my brood hen?"

"Oh." Hal didn't have a defense for that.

Absorbed in what they were doing, Emma and Hal forgot about the approaching storm until large, crystal clear drops pelted them. Emma dropped the hoe. A gust of wind caught the pile of seed packets, causing them to tumble over and over across the garden. Emma and Hal scrambled to gather up the remaining packets.

After Emma chased down the last packet, she yelled, "This is it. Run for the porch."

Leaning against the porch wall, Emma closed her eyes and turned her face toward the sky. "Ain't it something how a

74

spring shower keeps up making down? Smell the clean air and wet dust."

Hal stood beside her and looked out over the hay field and pasture. The shower draped the fields in a silver veil. She took a deep breath. "As clean as the smell of fresh-washed clothes drying on the line."

"Jah." Emma's tone changed. "Ach, nah! I forgot to bring in my clothes," she cried. As an after-thought she giggled. "Ach well, too late now. They will have to dry over." She looked across the yard at the darkened earth. Her voice filled with regret. "It's time to plant peas. As soon as the ground dries, I'll have to get that done."

"How do you know it's time to plant peas?"

"When the lilac bush leaves are as big as a mouse's ear," Emma said.

Hal had come to realize that Amish people tried to keep to an organized time-line with everything they did much like English people. Plain people use signs to do that with things that pertained to their rural life. English had forgotten how to do that. Her grandparents lived that way. That was years ago. Everyone goes by the calendar and their watches now instead of nature signs.

As quickly as the downpour started it ended. The overcast sky suddenly changed to sunshine. The sun caressed the earth and both of them with its light and warmth.

With excitement in her voice, Emma pointed. "Look a rainbow!"

The ethereal jewel-tone mist arched in the pasture just beyond the barn. "How lovely. As a child, I was told if I could find the end of the rainbow I'd find a pot of gold," Hal said.

"That's an English tale," Emma scoffed. "The rainbow came about because God made a promise to Noah. He said, "I have set my rainbow in the clouds, and it will be the sign of the covenant between me and the earth. Whenever I bring clouds over the earth and the rainbow appears in the clouds, I will remember my covenant between me and you and all living creatures of every kind. Never again will the waters become a flood to destroy all life." She paused, studying the rainbow before she continued. "If they feel the need to make wishes, English people should not wish for something that has to do with wealth."

Hal learned early on once she got to really know Emma, she should listen to this wise girl's thoughts. She was so very perceptive. Her insight into Amish life would be what was going to help Hal fit in. "What kind of wish, Emma?"

Emma paused to think before she spoke. "This could be many things. Maybe you should wish at the end of your rainbow to find happiness or health."

"Happiness. I like that wish. For quite a long time now, I've felt as if happiness is just out of my reach. If I wish on that rainbow, I'm going to have to wish really hard if I expect my wish to come true," Hal said softly.

Emma answered sagely, "Hallie, wishing for happiness does not make it happen. You have to work to get and keep happiness in your life. Now come with me. We have eggs to gather."

When Noah and Daniel came home from school, Emma was taking the eggs out of her bucket and placing them in a dark brown crock bowl. Without a word, she watched her brothers put their lunch pails on the counter.

The boys nodded a greeting at Hal. Very quietly, they headed for the mudroom to put on their knee boots.

"Not so fast. I want to talk to you," Emma said sharply.

The boys stopped and turned meekly to face her. She eyed them suspiciously. "I still can not find my rooster. Are you sure you do not know what has happened to him?"

Noah and Daniel shook their heads no.

"I can not understand why he is missing. Did you catch him for the Sunday dinner when we had fried chicken? Mind you if you did, that would not be a funny joke to me," Emma warned.

"Nah," Noah declared. "We would not do that."

"We know better than to harm your pet," Daniel assured her.

Hal felt sorry for the boys. They looked like they were telling the truth.

"It sure seems strange my rooster I have not seen since that very day," Emma said sharply, watching the boys closely. "Go on now and do the chores."

Noah and Daniel were good boys. Hal was sure they wouldn't have caught Zacchaeus to eat him. They wouldn't dare harm the chicken, knowing how much he meant to Emma. A bad feeling suddenly stirred in her gut. She thought of the rooster that walked up to her that Sunday morning she helped the boys butcher the roosters. He was a beauty, a dark wine red with long, black, arching tail feathers that shimmered emerald green when the sunlight hit them. He didn't seem afraid of her. At the time, she was sure he meant to fight her as most feisty roosters do. Could that have been Zacchaeus just looking for a handout from her as he would from Emma? The girl said her rooster hadn't been seen since that day.

That must have been what happened. Hal felt sick at her stomach. She rose from the table and peered out the window, hoping against hope that she was wrong. Yet so very sure she was right. What a terrible mess. It was all her fault that Emma's pet wound up on the Sunday dinner menu. How could she ever explain this to Emma? Killing a pet was not the way to become a trusted and beloved member of the Lapp family. If she found out, Emma would never forgive her for killing the pet rooster.

Oh, if only she hadn't let her pride get in the way. She should have told the boys she let the rooster get away from her. If she had, Noah would have understood and caught her another rooster. He'd have known to pick out a rooster that wasn't Zacchaeus. Oh sure, the boys might have teased her for not holding on to the rooster when he pecked her. That would have been far easier to take than having to live with what she had done to Zacchaeus. So much for thinking her wish on the rainbow might come true. Her happiness with this family had fallen victim to Noah's butcher ax along with the head of Zacchaeus.

It was close enough to milking time. She watched the boys hurry across the yard to the barn. They must be glad to get away from Emma's stern gaze. One more thing for her to regret. How could she ever live with herself if she let the boys take the blame for something so awful when she knew they were innocent?

Feeling guilty, Hal didn't have it in her to stay close to Emma in the kitchen. She was having trouble facing the girl with the dark secret she now carried. She had to have time to decide what she should do next. As she walked out of the kitchen, she said over her shoulder, "I'm going to the barn. I think I'll help the boys milk tonight."

Buttercat, the yellow tomcat, came to meet Hal when she opened the barn door. He wrapped himself around her ankles, tapping her with his twitching tail. His purr was so loud Hal could hear him above the generator hum. A couple of hens sat on top a pen door, cawing contently. Those two had every intention of spending the night right where they were. By morning, they might become some wild critter's meal. Hal walked around them and clapped her hands. The cackling hens flew down to the floor and raced out the open door. The last she saw of them, they were in a dead heat, going around the house on their way to the hen house.

Noah opened the back door to turn in the first set of ten cows.

One at a time, the cows burst into the barn. Large heads swinging and full utters swaying, each of the cows plodded for the same stanchion they stood in twice a day. Noah followed them. He slapped the first cow's bony flank to move her ahead enough to lock her neck into the stanchion. Spotting Hal, he asked, "Did you need something?"

"I just wanted to help milk," Hal said loud enough to carry over the generator motor. She carried Buttercat over to the closest straw-filled pen and put him down, hoping he'd stay out from underfoot. She went to the feed room and got the pail of dairy feed with a scoop laying on top. While Noah hooked up the milking cups, she walked in front of the cows, dispensing feed in the troughs. In seconds, milk surged through the clear plastic lines that ran above their heads and into the milk room bulk tank.

From the hayloft, Daniel called, "Look out below." He threw down a bale of alfalfa hay. It thudded against the barn floor, stirring up a large puff of dust. Daniel scrambled down the ladder and fished his pocket knife out to cut the strings. He gathered up an armload and backed the door open. "I am going to hay the horses and the bull," he told Hal.

The time passed by fast as they worked together. Hal leaned against the barn wall, arms folded over her chest. She watched Noah take the stainless steel milk cups off the last batch of cows. As she thought about facing Emma again, her dread grew heavier like a gunny sack full of potatoes on her back, trying to pull her down to her knees. Noah turned the generator off and started running the scoop shovel over the floor to clean it.

Daniel picked up a pail of shelled corn and oat mix in the feed room. "Come with me, Nurse Hal. We'll feed the sows."

On the way to the pig pen, Hal walked along with her hands in her denim jacket pockets, kicking at rocks in front of her.

"You look unhappy," Daniel surmised, looking up at her.

Either she was very transparent or Daniel was as perceptive as Emma. "That's because I am," she admitted.

Daniel looked concerned. "Why? Have we done something wrong?"

"No, but I sure did." Hal looked off over the hayfield, fighting back tears. "It's something that is going to make Emma mad at me. I mean really mad."

"I can not imagine Emma ever disapproving of you," Daniel scoffed.

"She will this time when she finds out," Hal assured him.

"What did you do?" Daniel asked, throwing the feed in

79

the trough on the other side the pig pen fence.

"I killed Zacchaeus."

Daniel pivoted around fast. His mouth flew open when he realized she was serious. The empty bucket slipped from his fingers, making a loud bang when it hit the ground. The pigs squealed in fear and backed away from the trough. Daniel was so busy studying Hal he didn't notice. "Why would you say that? I do not believe you could harm her rooster."

Hal's legs felt like rubber. She backed up, leaned against the pig pen fence and rested her elbows on the top board. She felt all color drain from her face as she asked, "Remember the day I helped you catch the roosters to fry for dinner?"

"Jah."

"When Noah and you left me alone, the rooster I had bit me. I dropped him. The rooster took off. I didn't want you to know that I couldn't succeed at such a simple task as holding onto a fryer for a few minutes. Another rooster walked right up to me. I figured he just wanted to be fed. I thought what luck. I grabbed at him and got him by the tail. I wouldn't have to bother Noah to catch another rooster. I was so proud of myself for catching a chicken by myself, but I didn't say anything to you. I didn't want you to know."

The full impact of Hal's story came to Daniel. "Oh, oh," he said softly.

"Emma thinks maybe you boys have the rooster hid some place. She's going to feel so bad when she finds out Zacchaeus is really dead," Hal said, tears running alongside her nose. "When she knows it was all my fault she will never like me again."

Noah called from the barn door, "What is taking so long?"

"Come here now. Quick!" Daniel said urgently, beckoning at his brother.

"What for?"

"Quick," Daniel repeated. He said softly to Hal, "We should ask Noah what to do."

80

Noah ran to them. Daniel explained Hal's problem. He suggested, "Maybe Nurse Hal should not say anything to Emma. She will give up looking for the rooster one of these days and find another one to make her a pet. What do you think, Noah?"

"One pet can never replace another. If something happened to Patches, do you think we will ever find another dog we would like as well?" Noah asked sagely.

"Oh," groaned Hal. "Noah is right, Daniel."

"You are not helping," Daniel warned Noah, rolling his eyes toward the upset woman.

A quick look at Hal and Noah could clearly see how bad she felt. He took her hand. "I think Emma will understand what you did was an accident."

Daniel grunted. "She would be much more forgiving of you than she would if it had been Noah and me that killed her rooster."

"Oh," Hal moaned. "That is another thing. If I don't tell Emma the truth, she'll go on thinking the two of you are guilty."

"As Daniel has said, if it is your wish to not tell her the truth we will not say anything about it. Emma will not worry for a long time. She will get busy and forget." Noah rolled his eyes at Daniel and said softly, "I hope."

"I don't know what to do." Hal wiped her eyes with her coat sleeve. "I feel so dishonest, but I don't want Emma to be mad at me."

Daniel took her other hand. "Emma will be sad for a little while if you tell her. That is all. It is the way of Plain people to forgive those who do something against us."

"I'd never intentionally do anything against any of you," protested Hal, sniffling. "I really didn't mean to kill Emma's pet. For her to forgive is one thing. What about forgetting?"

Noah shrugged as he patted her hand. "I think I can speak for Emma. Do not worry about us. You are like a mother to us. We know you could never do anything to hurt one of us."

Daniel perked up. "Can we ask her now, Noah?"

Hal sniffled and wiped her nose on the sleeve of her jacket. "Ask me what?"

"Daniel and me have been talking about what to call you. Nurse Hal does not seem right once you marry Daed. Daniel and I want to know if we can call you Mama Hal?" Noah asked.

Hal started crying again. She dropped to her knees and held her arms out to the boys for a hug. "At this moment, I don't feel I deserve such an honor, but I'd love you to call me Mama." As an after-thought, she said, "If it is all right with your father."

Emma stuck her head out the front door and yelled, "Supper is ready.

Hal wanted to be anywhere else at that moment rather in Emma's kitchen. She sighed. "Somehow I have to get up the courage to tell your sister the truth about Zacchaeus. Let me do it when I think the time is right."

The boys nodded they agreed.

Hal kept her eyes averted from Emma during supper. She was so uncomfortable with the awful secret she carried. What she did to the rooster kept boiling like a cauldron of bubbling hot chicken soup in her head. Her conscience bothered her like no other time in her life. How was she ever going to find the moment that was right to tell Emma she killed her pet rooster? She couldn't even look the girl in the eyes without wanting to cry. As upset as she was, this night was not the time to try to make a rational case for her awful deed. One that Emma would accept and forgive. If there was such a case.

Finally, that long, miserable evening was almost over. Emma wiped out the dishpan. She laid the dishcloth over the towel rack and dried her hands. "Now we are done. Hallie, sit down and talk to me. I sense something is bothering you. What is it?"

What made the Lapp children sense stuff like this, Hal wondered. She debated a second but just didn't have the guts to confess that she was Zacchaeus's murderer. That heaped on her worry about John spending too much time at Roseanna Miller's was almost more than she could bear. What if John decided to combine the Miller family and his since the Millers were Amish? That would be a marriage of convenience for the Lapp and Miller families that made more sense than John marrying her. Hal was sure John loved her. But no matter what his feelings were for her, he might think he would get a better bargain if he married this available Amish woman.

Hal didn't think she could stand it if she lost this family she loved. She had hoped to grow old with John and help raise his children. Maybe have some babies of her own.

Another idea kept nibbling at her. What if John couldn't pick between Roseanna and her? Right then she wished she knew everything there was to know about Amish beliefs. Did Amish men take more than one wife? If that was the case, she'd make it very clear to Mr. John Lapp, Hal Lindstrom would never become Amish enough to stand for that. She couldn't feel sorry enough for a pretty, young widow like Roseanna Miller to share her husband.

Hal keep her eyes on the dish towel she hung over the rack while she spoke, "I guess I worry too much. Your father is spending a lot of time with Roseanna Miller. I'm thinking John might decide it would be so much easier to bring an Amish woman into this family. Easier than it would be an English one. Especially a widow that is already a good homemaker.

"Daed would never do that to you. He loves you. He would never do that to his family. He knows his children love you like a mother," Emma declared.

Turning to Emma, Hal rubbed her throbbing forehead. "Tell me, do Amish men ever have more than one wife?"

Emma tried not to smile, but humor lit up her gray-green eyes. "Ach, Hallie. Nah, that is not permitted. You need not worry about such a thing. Stop such thoughts. My father loves you and no one else."

"I hope you're right." Hal felt so drained. She was on the verge of tears again. All she wanted right now was to be by herself. "I think I'll go home now. There are some things I've got to work out in my mind. Besides, I'm not fit company right now," Hal said, putting on her jacket.

She had so much to figure out. How was she ever going to get over being jealous of a widow who needed John's help? How was she ever going to tell Emma what happened to her pet rooster? That story was not going to add to her popularity with the Lapp family. With the uncertainty about where John stood with her, this was not a good time to get Emma upset with her. That girl had too much influence with her father. He really would lean in favor of taking Roseanna for his wife if Emma couldn't stand the sight of her.

All this worry was going to drive her crazy. She had to get home and try to get a better night's sleep than she did the night before. Surely everything would look less gloomy tomorrow morning if she wasn't so tired. Maybe then she could come up with some answers to her problems.

Later, John walked in the front door. He looked around the living room. Noah greeted him and jumped Daniel's black checker.

John said, "It sure is quiet in here. Hal's car is gone. I thought she might wait until I came home." He sounded disappointed that he missed seeing her.

"She left early," Noah shared, making another move with a red checker.

John glanced toward the dark kitchen. "Where is Emma?"

Eying his father, Daniel chirped, "She said she wanted to go to bed early, because she was tired."

Noah added, "She sounded mad if you ask me."

John tossed his straw hat at a wall peg. The hat bounced off the peg and slid down the wall to the floor. He plopped down on the couch close to the boys. "I have not been around much lately. I feel as if I have missed what is going on at home. Mind if I ask if there is anything I should know about?"

Noah and Daniel wrinkled their noses at each other.

"You say," Daniel told his brother.

"Maybe you should ask Emma what is bothering her,"

Noah said. As an after thought he warned, "Do not stand too close to her. She is not easy to be around when she is upset."

"All recht, I will remember," John said. He pushed himself off the couch slowly with an effort. His days had been long and tiresome since he took over the Miller chores. All he wanted to do was to go to bed and be rested enough to start over in the morning. Maybe tomorrow night would have a better ending. Hal would be waiting for him when he got home.

He trod up the stairs. As much as he wanted to turn in his bedroom door, he went past and knocked on Emma's.

"What is it?" Emma asked tersely.

"Sorry if I woke you up," he said.

"You did not wake me," she replied sharply.

"Can I talk to you?" John asked tentatively.

"Jah, Daed."

John crossed as far as the foot of her bed, thinking about Noah's warning. He stared through the dark, trying to make out his daughter's head. "You went to bed early. Are you sick?"

"Just worried. To worry makes me tired," she said shortly.

"What worries you?"

Emma shot up to a sitting position. "Daed, I fear you are going to lose Hallie if you do not talk to her about what you do at Roseanna's farm. She is uneasy because you stay with Roseanna and her family for supper. She asked me tonight if Amish men ever have two wives."

"She did?" He could not imagine Hal thinking about such a thing.

"She did."

"Do you think she would approve of marrying a man that has another wife?" John asked, bewildered.

"You know she would not. But she worries that you might think that way. Hallie does not understand our ways. Little by little, she asks about our beliefs. I told her not to worry herself with such a thought. You only wanted to marry her," Emma drew out, feeling drained.

"Gute. That is settled."

Emma plopped back onto the bed. She crossed her arms over her chest, letting out a discussed gust of air. "Nothing is settled. Hearing it from me is not the same as you telling Hallie. She worries so much she does not feel pretty good. Her eating has gone away. She don't look too good in the face, either."

"It is that bad, ain't?"

"Jah," Emma snapped.

"All recht. Denki for telling me," John said with a feeling of irritation rising in him.

"Talk to her soon, Daed. Do not let her worry for very much longer. It is not a gute thing for all of us," Emma warned.

"I will do that Emma. Now get some rest," he told her.

I will have a talk with Hal soon, he told himself in the hall. The short distance John trudged to his bedroom, his feet felt like pieces of heavy lead. He would not have the kind of talk Emma wanted, but he wasn't going to tell his daughter that. He didn't want to have her on his bad side right away. Emma had become a mother hen to Hal. It would only take a few words from him to get his daughter to side with Hal. So he'd risk Emma being cross with him after he talked to Hal. That English woman had to understand that Plain people helped each other in order to survive in their community. She would be expected to do the same thing when she became Amish. John leaned against his doorway and stared into his dark bedroom. This trouble would not be happening if I could have convinced Hal to move in with me. Maybe she would not be thinking such thoughts about Roseanna if she was in my bed waiting for me at this very minute.

He punched the door facing. What is wrong with Hal? He thought about why she'd act this way. It came to him. Hal was jealous. That was it. For the life of him, he didn't know why. Hadn't he told her he loved her often enough?

John sat down on the bed and removed one of his high topped farmer shoes. The shoe plunked on its side by the bed. She has to know I would never do anything to destroy what we

86

have together. He'd talk to her all right. He removed the other shoe and gave it a hard toss, bouncing it off the other one.

She had to change her way of thinking before they married. If Hal Lindstrom couldn't see this his way, there would be no marriage. That's what he would tell her, then he'd take his chances with Emma.

Chapter 8

The next afternoon, Hal was delighted when she finally had a patient show up at the clinic. For some reason, when he walked in she felt she'd met the man before. Broad shouldered and medium built, he had kind blue eyes. His full head of sandy, bushy hair frayed out from under his straw hat, but he didn't have a beard. That meant he wasn't married.

Hal held out her hand to him. "Good afternoon. I'm Nurse Hal. What can I do for you?"

Hesitating, he stared at her before he shook her hand. Finally, he found his voice. "I am Samuel Nisley. This morning my arm I skinned. The sore keeps sticking to my sleeve."

"Ouch! Sit down at the table. I'll take a look at it." As Samuel laid his arm on the table, Hal asked, "Have we met before?"

"We passed on the road once maybe," Samuel said, his bright blue eyes twinkling with amusement.

Where she saw him came back to Hal. She closed her eyes and took a deep breath. "You were the one at the intersection that had such a good time watching John's horse go in circles."

"Jah." Recollection of that moment made Samuel's face crinkle into a smile. "I'm sorry I laughed at you. Looked like you could not guide the buggy very pretty gute. It sort of went

88

wvertzwaerrici in the road." He noticed the questioning look on Hal's face. "Sorry. Crosswise."

"That was the horse's idea, not mine," Hal excused. She poured saline solution on the shirt sleeve to soften up the dried stained area stuck to the skin tear. In a minute, the shirt should come loose easier.

"Why did you not say whoa?" Samuel asked.

"That was John's fault. He said let the horse do the driving for me. I thought Ben would know what he was supposed to do. Guess not, huh?" She grinned then went to work on his arm. Hal slowly and carefully rolled the light blue shirt sleeve up and pulled the material away from the skin tear. "That is a large tear. It's a good thing you came. How did you do this?"

Samuel said sheepishly, "Tripped and fell into the barn door. Caught my arm on a hinge."

"You really should have a tetanus shot to prevent lockjaw. You'll have to go to a doctor for the shot," Hal said, setting her supplies on the table. Though the large area of puckered skin had started to dry, she worked the skin gently back over the raw area with a Q tip. After she placed butterfly strips along the torn edge, she instructed, "I'm putting gauze loosely on the area so you don't get it dirty. The gauze should be changed every day for a few days. At night, you can leave it off to let the area air. If you see redness around the wound, come back."

Suddenly from behind her, Emma hissed, "Hallie, Hallie."

Hal looked over her shoulder to see why the girl sounded like a tire with a slow leak.

Emma's head was stuck in the clinic doorway. She whispered, "I wanted to warn you Stella Strutt is here."

Outside, heavy footsteps pounded up the steps. Hal stiffened at the sound, but she kept working on the bandage. She glanced at her patient's face. Samuel was watching her much too close to her liking. On top of facing a disagreeable, unlikeable old woman much too often to suit her, she now had the scrutiny of a patient. A blind man could have sensed she was uneasy about being anywhere near Stella. She could only hope this visit in front of Samuel went well. The door burst open. The heavy set, black, foreboding form, with what seemed to be a permanent scowl plastered on her face, filled the opening. At least, Hal couldn't remember ever seeing a pleasant expression on that woman's face.

Trying to shove the feeling of dread back that crossed her face, Hal cleared her throat and made her voice sound welcoming. "Please come in, Stella."

"Ouch," Samuel utter under his breath.

Hal turned her attention to her patient. "I'm sorry. Did I hurt you?"

He grimaced. "You are getting the tape a little tight on the bandage. Could you loosen it up once?"

Hal felt bad when she looked at the paper tape wound in layers tightly around Samuel's arm. The man's hand had already turned pink. Quickly, Hal cut the tape, threw away the gauze and started over. This time she concentrated on what she was doing. "I'm so sorry, Samuel. Is this better?" She asked, checking the tape and the color of his hand.

Samuel clasped Hal's hand in his strong, large, calloused one. He darted a glance at Stella's back and whispered, "I understand. We all get the jitters at some time or other in our life."

"Thank you," Hal said softly as she looked over her shoulder in search of Emma. The clinic door was closed. Emma, like a rat leaving the danger of a sinking battleship, had disappeared.

Stella's wide, heavy soled, black oxfords pounded the floor as she walked across the room. Ignoring Hal, she took a broad stance in front of the farmer. "Samuel Nisley, nice to see you."

"Been a while," he said politely.

"Jah. Came to see what this clinic looked like. Looked like indeed. Is all the talk at church meetings." She turned her back to Hal and scrutinized the room, her arms folded over her ample chest.

Stella's swelled, dimpled feet spilled over her shoes. How did the woman walk on those painful feet? Trying to be sympathetic, Hal said, "Mrs. Strutt, you're welcome to sit down and visit."

From outside came the roar of a truck motor. Patches gave his company's here bark. Hal heard the ominous sound made by screeching tires and the ping of flying gravel scattering about. That was followed by a long, loud, pain filled yelp.

If those scary sounds weren't enough, Daniel's piercing scream filled Hal with fear.

The scream was followed by Noah's scared voice crying, "Mama Hal. Mama Hal."

Hal yanked the door open. She ran out on the porch with Samuel and Stella right behind her. The milk truck was parked by the barn with the cab door open. The driver, a heavy set middle aged man, sat on the truck step holding his head in his hands. Had he hit one of the boys?

Noah and Daniel ran to her. She met them halfway in the driveway. "What's wrong?" Hal called. She grabbed each of them by a shoulder, inspecting them. "Are you all right?"

Daniel launched himself at her as he wailed, "Mama Hal, the milkman ran over our dog." He pointed to Patches. That's when Hal saw him. Her stomach turned over at the sight. The dog's motionless, crumpled body lay in a bloody pile just behind the milk truck's front tire.

Her heart thumping, Hal walked with the boys to look at the dog. It was clear there wasn't anything to be done for Patches. He was already gone. She glanced at the driver. The poor man looked so miserable. She whispered, "Noah and Daniel, this was an accident. Look at the driver. He feels as bad as you do."

As if he realized their whispers were about him, the driver looked up and into their grieving eyes. "I'm really sorry about this, boys. Your dog came out of nowhere. I couldn't stop quick enough," he bemoaned. His eyes glimmered with moisture.

Noah took a deep breath. "We know you could not help it, Mr. Johnson."

"For days now, Patches has been running at my car when I drive in. I've been afraid it would be me that hit him" said Hal, commiserating with the milkman. "We're sorry it had to happen to you."

As the milkman said he appreciated Hal and the boys understanding, Samuel and Emma walked up behind her. Her hand at her throat, Emma squatted down to look at Patches.

Samuel said solemnly, "I am leaving now."

Hal wiped at the tears spilling down her cheeks. "Don't forget you should go to the doctor for a tetanus shot. Oh, and be sure to let me or Emma check your arm if it looks red."

Seeing how upset Hal and the children were, Samuel's mind wasn't on his arm. "Where is John today?" His voice was filled with concern.

Only half listening, Hal's mind was on how to help the boys take in the loss of their dog. She said abstractly, "If he isn't in the field, he's doing chores at Roseanna Miller's farm. He does her milking now that her husband has passed away."

Hal knelt beside Patches. She felt the rocks poke through her blue jeans and dig into her knees. That pain didn't begin to describe the way she felt inside when she looked at the dog's lifeless body. Hal scooped him up in her arms and held him close. By the time she walked over to lay the dog gently down in the grassy shade by the barn, Samuel was leaving. Hal watched the Amish man turn his buggy around and head out of the driveway.

Stella Strutt's wide soled shoes thudded as she stepped heavily, coming down the porch steps. The woman heaved herself into her buggy and waited her turn to leave.

Hal said to the children, "Let's go sit on the porch for a moment and catch our breath. We need to talk about this."

"Hallie, you have blood all over your clothes," stated Emma, her eyes tearful.

Licking her dry lips, Hal looked down at her blouse. "I

don't mind."

As they started toward the house, Stella Strutt pulled away. Hal was glad that woman left. It was a relief not to have to deal with the difficult woman at a time like this. She couldn't handle the affect Patches death was having on her and the children and Stella Strutt at the same time. That would have been too much to bear.

The four of them lined up on the top porch step. Tears rolled down Noah and Daniel's faces. Emma looked sad. They hugged their knees and eyed the black and white heap by the barn.

Hal had to do something to help them. "We have to have a funeral for Patches. Don't you think?"

"Jah," Daniel said, making a swipe under his nose with his sleeve.

Emma asked, "Where can we bury Patches?"

Noah said solemnly, "In the picnic grove."

"Wonderful idea." Hal studied her bloody hands. "First, I have to wash up a bit. We have a funeral to plan."

In the kitchen, she rubbed her hands together in the wash pan, staining the water red. After she got rid of the bloody liquid out the back door, she dumped another dipper in the empty pan. This time she used a wash cloth to dab at her blouse. All the water did was smear the blood, making the wet spots bigger and brighter. Leaning against the counter for support, Hal dried her hands. She bit her lower lip, trying not to cry. It wouldn't do the children any good to see her lose it. As the adult she had to be the strong one. She had peroxide in the clinic. Pouring some of that on the blouse would fade the blood away.

"Nurse Hal, come help us quick," Daniel cried. His emotional voice came from a distance.

"Nah, do not take Patches," Noah wailed.

"Now what?" She rushed out the door.

Emma hugged the porch post with a tight grip. She sagged at the knees as if she was too weak to stand up. Out in the driveway, Noah groaned loudly. Beside him, Daniel, hands over his face, sobbed hard again.

Hal ran to them. "What's wrong?"

The boys pointed toward the barn. The Lapp buggy was parked where the milk truck had been. At first sight, Hal felt relief that John was home. Then he stepped from behind the horse and buggy. Her relief turned to anger.

John had picked up the dog. He held Patches upside down. The limp dog dangled from his hand by the back legs. As John moved away from the barn, blood ran from the dog's nose and mouth, turning the grass red.

"Mama Hal, Daed is taking Patches away," Daniel whimpered.

The little boy's voice was enough to push Hal into action. She rushed across the driveway. Noah was on one side and Daniel on the other, trouping along with her. Emma closed the ranks behind as the four of them circled out around John's buggy. The horse's head came up. His ears twitched back as they rushed by him. The animal gave them a wild-eyed look and fidgeted in his traces.

"John, where are you going with our dog?" Hal demanded, making sure to keep her voice low. She had learned one lesson lately. She didn't want to excite the horse any more than he already was.

As his family and Hal confronted him, John looked surprised and wary. "Going to get rid of him."

"Get rid of him?" Hal repeated shrilly.

"Jah, throw him in the gully back of the pasture."

Emma gasped. Her hands flew to her pale face.

"Nah," Daniel whimpered, grabbing Hal's hand.

"Stop him, Nurse Hal," Noah said hoarsely.

John looked from one to the other, confused by their reaction. He said flatly, "Kids, the dog's dead."

"You just can't throw our dog away," Hal said, tears running down her face. She held her hands out to take the dog from him. "Give Patches to me."

"You will get ----." He stopped when his eyes focused on her blouse. He realized it was too late to warn her about getting blood on her clothes. Shaking his head in bewilderment, John gently laid Patches in her arms as he repeated softly, "He's dead, Hal. You can not make him better."

"We know that. The children and I are going to have a funeral for him. We want to bury him," Hal explained. "You can't just throw Patches in a ditch and leave him for the coyotes to eat. What are you doing home this time of day anyway?"

A painful look covered John's face. "Samuel Nisley came to the Miller farm. He told me what happened. He said you and the children needed me. He's milking Roseanna's cows tonight."

"Oh," Hal said in a small voice. She'd been right about Samuel. He was a kind man. She had seen it in his eyes. Her tone stung John like rusted barbed wire, deeply biting into his soul. Rather than be glad of her ability to hurt him, she felt worse that she had spoken before she thought. The children needed their father right now. She needed him. But then she had needed him for days that he hadn't been around. That didn't give her the right to be spiteful to him. She shouldn't have taken out her sadness about Patches on him.

She looked somewhere over John's shoulder and asked, "In that case, do you want to come to Patches's funeral?"

John looked at each of the sad faces in front of him with a beleaguered expression in his eyes. "Jah, I am part of this family, too."

"Please, get a shovel. We're going to the picnic grove," Hal ordered as she turned on her heels. "Emma, bring an old towel or sheet to use for a shroud. Noah, run ahead and pick us out a burial site."

Supper was strained. No one was hungry. John's words kept running over and over in Hal's mind. I am part of this family, too. His feelings had been hurt by her surprised reaction to his coming home early from the Miller farm. Not that the children noticed. They were too upset over the death of their dog. Well, she knew how they felt. She was going to miss Patches as much as they did.

After kitchen cleanup, Hal had it in her mind to tell John she was leaving. She found he had fallen asleep in his rocker while reading his bible. She really didn't want to wake him. Right now she wasn't fit company. She felt guilty about snapping at him earlier. The main thing was he was home, and the children had their father tonight. They didn't need her. She slipped quietly across the living room so she wouldn't wake John.

Hal wondered how she'd gotten herself so far down in the dumps? What started out as a tiny seed of discontent about John spending too much time with Roseanna had bloomed into the ugliest of grasshopper eaten thistles. She hated this feeling of distrust that nagged her about John. She wanted to believe he didn't deserve the way she was treating him.

Hal's hand was on the cold, metal doorknob.

"Whoa! I want to talk to you," John snapped.

The chilly feel of that metal matched John's icy voice. By the time she turned around, John was removing his bible from his lap and one of Emma's potholders. Hal glanced toward the kitchen door, but Emma was out of sight. As he crossed the room, John's expression was unreadable. Hal, not talking, not moving, watched him come with an ominous feeling that she was in trouble.

"I want to talk to you alone before you leave. Come out on the porch with me." He held the door open for her. Hal sat down on edge of the porch and John joined her. He steepled his fingers together and looked toward the barn. "You would have left without waking me."

"Yes, I know how tired you are. Besides, I felt bad for having snapped at you this afternoon. I am sorry I did that," Hal apologized.

"Your tone just made me sure that we need to discuss what is wrong between us. This will not be the last time I help my neighbors in times of need. I know that they would do the same for me. This is the way we live our lives. Between chores, farming and doing my part to help neighbors, my days are filled. You have to realize my way of life will not change

96

because you are a part of it. You have to be the one to adjust. Work alongside me. Take up the slack in this family when I am not here and always trust me as I trust you. If you can not do that, a marriage between us will not work," he said plainly. His gaze fastened on her face.

"I want to marry you," Hal said sincerely.

"Gute. I fear that being an Amish wife will not be easy for you. We believe Christ is the head of man, and man is the head of woman. Men assume the responsibility that God has placed on their shoulders as head of the family to make all decisions. Not to accept that responsibility is to lie down on my job, to fail God's will. Do you understand me?" John asked firmly.

Hal's eyes narrowed. "We have a problem! Are you telling me you are the boss about everything in the marriage. I am to obey your every wish and can't think for myself?"

"That is our way," John said with a grimace. "Men go through the doors first and are thought of first about everything before their wives and children."

"I wasn't brought up that way. I expect to be free to express my opinions. Your way sets women back a century. I don't know if I can agree to this," Hal said with uncertainty.

John's ultimatum was clear. "If you agree to convert to Amish, you must accept all of our ways. You must decide to live our way before we marry. If you can not agree, we can not marry."

"Can I have a few days to think about this?"

"Jah, think and be sure about what is recht for you, Hal. I do not want another unhappy wife again," he said. He stood and held his hand out to help her up. "I will walk you to your car."

"Is that permitted?" Hal asked sarcastically.

John eyed her as he said flatly, "If it is what I choose to do."

"Well, tonight I think I will go alone to my car. We're not married yet. It is what I choose to do. Good night," Hal said flippantly as she marched away from him.

Chapter 9

The next afternoon, Hal had her elbows propped on the table in the clinic, trying to work through the fight she'd had with John. He seemed so rigid. Was there any way for her to get him to bend the rules? She was her own person, No one, not even her husband was going to make decisions for her or speak for her.

Emma swished into the room and broke the silence. "It's a perfect day for a ride. The buggy's all ready to go. Come with me, Hallie."

"Guess we could be gone for awhile. Doesn't look like we're needed around here." Hal smiled at the girl and amended, "I'll go providing you do the driving."

Emma laughed. "I'd be glad to drive just so we get where we are going. I hear you like to drive the horse in circles. That would get us no where fast."

"Very funny. No matter what your father told you, that was all the horse's idea. I assure you," Hal said as she climbed into the enclosed buggy. "Where are we going?"

"I thought we could go visit Roseanna Miller," Emma said casually.

"Why?" Hal asked sharply.

Emma clucked to the horse and flicked the lines over his back to get him started. "It is the custom to visit a family

98

that has lost a loved one as often as we can so they know they are not alone. I have not done that once yet. It is time that I did."

"Looks to me like your father does enough visiting with Roseanna for the whole family," cracked Hal, looking out her window.

"We feel sorry for Roseanna and her children." With her eyes on the road, Emma chided, "We should show it."

Knowing she wasn't going to convince Emma to doubt her father, Hal gave in. "You are right as usual."

A light gray spiral of smoke floated from the Miller chimney. The odor of fresh baked goods surrounded Emma and Hal as they stepped onto the porch. Emma knocked. Inside came the heavy thud of rushing footsteps on the hardwood floor.

With a big smile, Roseanna, in her widow's black, welcomed Hal and Emma. "Welcome. It is so gute to see you. We are working in the kitchen."

She waited for them to hang their jackets on the wood rack pegs along the living room wall. Homemade throw rugs lay about on the living room's hardwood floor. Some square, loom woven rugs and others were braided ovals. On the hard floor, the rugs made soft spots to walk on.

Jimmy and Ella, at the kitchen table, leaned over a big circle of rolled out dough. They looked up when the company came in. The children nodded bashfully at Hal, but they had big smiles for Emma.

Roseanna said, "We are making doughnuts today. Do not look too closely at my children. When they help me they are fershmeerd with flour." She took up the end of her black apron and rubbed Ella's flour covered cheeks.

Emma hugged Ella and patted Jimmy's head. "Maybe they are as gute to eat as the doughnuts."

"No, not near as gute as doughnuts," Jimmy assured her.

"Roseanna, we are sorry to have taken so long to come visit," Emma said. "The time flies by me too fast some days."

99

"That is all right," the woman said softly. "Please, sit down." She pinched the dough as she said shyly, "Emma, I do not know if you have noticed but John has a sweet tooth. I am making extra doughnuts. You can take some home for him. But make sure he shares with all of you."

Emma exclaimed, "How nice. What a treat! The minute Noah and Daniel sniff out your doughnuts, Daed will have no choice but to share."

Laughing, Roseanna turned to her children. She said something in Dutch. Jimmy and Ella tore bits of dough off and shaped them into balls.

"I do not know what we would have done without John's kind help," said Roseanna, checking the grease filled fryer on the wood cook stove.

Hal tensed slightly and looked at the round, white, battery operated clock on the wall. She wasn't sure how much longer she could put up with compliments about John from Roseanna. As far as she was concerned, Emma and she had stayed long enough. She was ready to leave.

Emma placed her hand on Hal's as she addressed Roseanna. "My father is only too happy to help."

"The grease is hot enough, Ella and Jimmy," Roseanna said. She dropped a few pieces of dough into the fryer as the kids handed them to her.

The grease sizzled as the doughnuts fried, making the kitchen smell of heated lard and sugar pastry. Roseanna pushed the dough around in the grease with a spoon. She said to Hal, "John was so nice to let you put the clinic onto his home."

Hal stared at Roseanna until Emma elbowed her. "Yes, it was nice of John."

Too busy to notice Hal's uneasiness, Roseanna went on, "It is gute of you to share your time and talents with the Plain community. We have needed someone like you here for a long time."

Roseanna set a plate of hot doughnuts on the table. There didn't look as if there was much difference in the golden brown delicacies from bakery doughnuts except they didn't have holes. As soon as the doughnuts cooled, Roseanna covered one side of them with a rich white frosting made from powdered sugar. "Now eat all you want while the doughnuts are warm. I'll pour you a cup of coffee. Some people like to dunk their doughnuts."

Begrudgingly, Hal had to admit she'd never tasted a doughnut this delicious. She liked bakery doughnuts but Roseanna's were much better. "Thank you for the treat, Roseanna. These are very good."

"I am glad you like them, Nurse Hal. I hope you come back often to visit, but I can not promise to have doughnuts every time," Roseanna said and laughed.

On the way home, Emma said, "Did you think Roseanna is a nice woman?"

"She is," Hal said.

"You see why my father would want to help her and her children?"

"Yes, I see," agreed Hal. What was she supposed to say? A person would have to be heartless not to think Roseanna Miller was a nice woman who needed a man around at chore time. What she thought of Roseanna wasn't the point. What worried Hal most was what John Lapp thought of the young, pretty Widow Miller. As if all her assets weren't enough, Hal could add one more to the list that would appeal to John. She was an Amish woman who, unlike Hal, would be an obedient servant if he married her.

At home, Hal followed Emma into the kitchen and leaned against the door facing. Emma dropped the wax paper bundle of doughnuts on the table. Her mind was on gathering eggs and getting supper.

"Emma, I don't think I can stay for supper tonight. I'm going back to town," said Hal.

The girl picked the egg bucket up and set it back down. She leaned against the table and folded her arms, ready to persuade Hal she shouldn't leave. "Stay and talk to Daed when he comes in. You will feel better once you have seen him."

"I don't think it will help. He seems to have his mind

101

on all he has to do here and at the Miller farm these days. Besides, we have talked. Your father made it clear to me the way he feels and thinks. I just don't know what he can say to make me see things like he does," Hal said in an exasperated tone.

"Hallie, didn't you see him in the field when we drove by on the way to the Miller farm? Now he is home, helping Noah and Daniel with the milking. He did not do Roseanna's chores tonight," pointed out Emma.

"Is he in the barn? I didn't notice. Why is he home?" Hal asked curiously.

"Samuel Nisley has taken over milking the Miller cows for a while. If Daed listens to you would you be willing to talk to him again? Tell him how you feel. Say out loud the thoughts you are thinking that make you miserable," insisted Emma.

"Sure. But John isn't going to be willing to listen to me so why wait. I just want to go home. Good night, Emma."

Thinking she probably shouldn't have bothered to come to the farm after their fight last night, she walked to the edge of the porch and froze. John was at the bottom of the steps, looking up at her. He paused for a minute searching her face. For what she didn't know. He started up the steps.

"Are you leaving so soon? I am ready to come in for the night. The boys are going to finish the milking. I can spend some time with you tonight," He said tentatively as he stopped in front of her a few steps down. He shoved his hands in his pockets and looked up at her, waiting for her answer.

"I'm feeling tired. I'm going home." Hal stepped sideways to go around him.

John stepped sideways to get in front of her again. "You call your apartment home yet? I had hoped you thought of my home as yours by now. We need to talk."

"I haven't decided yet where my home is." Hal moved over to go around him.

John moved in front of her again. "Mind standing still and listening to me, Hal?" He stepped up to the step in front of her and put his hands on her shoulders to hold her in place.

"Can you not give me a chance to talk about what is wrong between us?"

From a crack in the door came Emma's assertive voice. "Jah, she will. She said she would if you asked."

Looking back over her shoulder, Hal hissed, "Sh, Emma!"

"You just told me if Daed wanted to talk you would listen," Emma said sticking her head out the door.

"Did you say that?" John asked with a hopeful look.

"Sort of. I think what Emma said was if I wanted to talk you would listen to ----," Hal didn't finish. A buggy turned into the driveway. "You have company."

John glanced over his shoulder. He turned back to her and grasped her hand. "Elton and Jane Bontrager. Please stay until they leave. We must talk after they are gone."

"All right. I'll stay," she agreed.

"I want you to meet Jane Bontrager. She will want to meet you.

Welcome," he called to the Bontragers as they climbed out of their buggy. As the older couple came across the yard, John said, "Jane, meet Nurse Hal."

Smiling, Jane shook Hal's hand. "I have heard a lot about you. It is gute to meet you."

Elton nodded at Hal. As John turned to escort them into the house, Elton touched his arm. "Before we go in, I want you to look at this new horse I bought. I'm not so sure I got a gute bargain."

"I will do that. Hal take Jane inside," John said as he followed Elton to the buggy.

Hal held the door for Jane to enter, watching the men walk away from them. Emma peeped around the door from the kitchen. She set the egg bucket on the floor and pointed to the couch. "Welcome, Jane. Sit down."

Emma sat down next to Jane. Hal chose a chair next to the couch. As she glanced out the window while Jane and Emma talked, she tuned out their conversation. Absorbed with John and Elton by the Bontrager buggy, she wished she could read lips.

John faced Elton with his hands in his pant pockets. From the long looks on their faces, Hal figured this had to be a serious discussion. One thing she knew for sure, the subject couldn't be about Elton's new horse. She'd seen plenty of western movies. This wasn't the way John Wayne checked a horse. He would have pulled up the horse's upper lip to see his teeth. Wayne would have ran his hand up and down the horse's legs and raised the horse's hooves to see the bottoms. She didn't have a clue what he'd be looking for, but if John Wayne inspected a horse that way, it had to be right. Something was wrong. Elton wanted John away from his family to discuss it.

Hal had a grim feeling this was a sign Elton wasn't visiting as a friend but as the bishop. Maybe there had been too much gossip about John being helpful to Roseanna Miller. Seemed to her when the Amish folks gathered, they were more than happy to talk about anything and everybody. Maybe Elton wanted to know John's intentions. Hal wished she knew the answer to that herself. Perhaps Roseanna went to Elton on her own behalf, wishing for him to speak to John about marriage. As long as the bishop had the final word, Hal's future with the Lapp family might be looking pretty bleak after the men finished their talk.

When John turned his attention to the horse, Elton put a hand on his arm. "Gute to see you, John. We have not had much time to talk since we built the clinic. Spring planting done?"

"Jah and yours?"

"Jah, I am done." Elton licked his lips nervously. "John, someone has brought something to my attention. I wanted to speak privately of this matter to you."

"I knew something was wrong. You have the best horse sense of anyone I know. I did not think you would need my opinion," John stated knowingly. "What has happened?"

"Stella Strutt came to see me about a matter of concern to her. As you may realize when Stella has a concern it is always a very large problem to her," Elton said.

"What is wrong now?" John asked, exasperated at the very mention of that woman.

Emil paused to look toward the house. "She was here recently to see the clinic."

John raised an eyebrow. "Was she?"

"Jah, the day your dog was killed."

"That day was a bad time for Hal and my children. They were upset. I do not see what would have bothered Stella about that," John defended.

"Her concern was that I should ask you to tell Nurse Hal to leave and not come back. She wants the clinic done away with," Elton said.

"Why?"

"She said that day your sons called Nurse Hal Mama. She felt Nurse Hal is just to be here for the clinic. This familiarity should not be permitted. John Lapp's sons should not be calling an English woman by this term," Elton related.

"Ach," uttered John, ramming his hands into his pants pocket.

"I told Stella I would look into the matter. At first, I was puzzled by what she said. The more I thought about it, the clearer it became to me. Nurse Hal spends much time here. Only a blind person would miss the signs of fondness between you and her. I can see the children are fond of her, too," Elton told him.

John's voice didn't reveal anything when he said, "Jah, go on."

"You would not go to the trouble to build a room onto your house to use for a clinic unless you were sure Nurse Hal would be here to use this clinic for a long time. Am I right?"

"Jah, that is the plan," John agreed, nudging a clump of grass with the toe of his shoe.

Leaning his head to one side, Elton ran his hand over his beard. "I recalled a time in the winter when Emma walked over to visit. She was full of questions about an English friend that might want to convert to Amish. All of these signs together seemed to add up to be serious enough for me to check out

105

Stella's concern. I have to know what is going on now that Stella has voiced her disapproval."

John gave him a direct look. "I have asked Hal to marry me. She has agreed. We will need your approval when we are ready."

"I thought as much, but I needed to hear it from you. John, you are as honest as the day is long. I knew you would tell me the truth if I asked. We do not announce a wedding until two weeks before the event. In this situation, there much for Nurse Hal to do. A discussion with me about her converting to Amish and the classes each person takes before hand. When you and Nurse Hal are ready to talk to me, you will have to come see me before your announcement in church. I will make my decision after I have talked to her," Elton said.

"What about Stella Strutt?"

Elton scratched his temple just below his straw hat. "Sometimes God calms the storm, but sometimes God lets the storm rage and calms his child."

John had a humorous glint in his eyes. "Which is Hal? The storm or the child?"

Elton snorted. "This should not surprise you. Stella Strutt is the storm. She has been a large, dark cloud raining over this community for a long time."

"Thank you for that." John managed a slight grin.

"Sometimes Hal feels like the storm to me. Our ways are puzzling to her yet. It does not help that somehow she always seems to upset Stella or the other way around."

"If Stella's problem wasn't Nurse Hal it would be something else. Stella will listen to me. She will not like it, but she knows my word is final. I will tell her we need Nurse Hal to run this clinic. We are lucky to have her. Your children do not have a mother, and Nurse Hal supplies that need while she is here. I am willing to overlook she is English as long as the Lapps want her here," Elton said firmly.

John looked doubtful. "You think that will be enough to settle Stella down without mentioning our intention to get married?"

106

"It is true the woman is very strong-minded. She is a no-nonsense person that sees everything in her life only from her way of thinking. That may be all right with her family, but I do not always want to have her push her stubborn determination on me or to butt into other people's business. She must not be allowed to think she can will me to think the way she does. As Bishop, I have to make up my own mind about what is right," Elton said sternly.

"You may be sorry for not doing as she asks," John warned.

"Nah, she knows that I have the last word here. She will abide by what I say."

"If she finds out about our marriage, if you permit it, she won't like it," John warned.

Elton licked his lips. "I do not intend to tell her. It is the custom to keep an intended marriage a secret between families until just before the wedding. That will give you time to make sure this is what you and Nurse Hal want. Stella will find out in church with everybody else and have very little time to form an objection."

"Denki for understanding," John said gratefully.

"If I decide to allow your marriage, I hope by the time Stella finds out, she will be so surprised she will not have time to react before the impending wedding ceremony," Elton said with a wry smile.

"Denki, Bishop," John said. "Does Jane know about Stella's visit to you?"

Elton smiled and said wisely, "He who has a secret of this nature dares not tell it to his wife until the time is right. No, she does not know yet."

John darted a glance toward the house then back at Elton. "If it is all right with you, I would like to keep this our secret for a while. Hal has been nervous enough lately about what is ahead of her without having to contend with Stella's unfriendliness."

"I agree," said Elton. "Now let's go inside and see what the women are up to."

107

Chapter 10

Jane was saying, "Emma, Elton tells me you have a pet rooster."

At the mention of the rooster, Hal put her attention on their conversation.

She hated the sad reaction on Emma's face at the mention of her pet. "I did have, but he disappeared."

"Sorry to hear that. Chickens have a short life what with the critters catching them," Jane said.

As usual with her half full disposition, Emma made a stab at brightening up the conversation. "How about having a piece of cake with us, Jane? I just baked a raisin spice one."

"Sounds voonderball gute even if it is close to supper time," Jane said.

Emma headed for the kitchen. "Come help me, Hallie."

Once through the kitchen door, Hal whispered, "Something is wrong, isn't it? Elton isn't here just to visit. He's here as the bishop. Otherwise, he wouldn't have kept John outside so long where we couldn't hear what they said."

"Seems so," Emma said calmly, placing plastic blue bowls and silverware on the table. "Bring the cake in from the cold room."

Whatever was wrong was something that was going to affect her. Hal just knew it was. She was sure she wasn't going to like it. Quickly, she picked up the metal cake pan and turned to go back to the kitchen. The cool pan flew from her trembling, clammy hands. The cake landed upside down on the floor with a splat and tinny sound of metal versus floor.

What a mess. What was she going to do now? Emma wasn't going to like this. Hal remembered her mother used to say Aunt Tootie's floor was always clean enough to eat off. Well, so was Emma's, and she promised Jane a piece of cake. Quickly, Hal squatted and slowly turned the cake pan over. The cake, glued to the floor by the white frosting, was a cracked disaster of pieces and crumbs. She picked the chunks up and carefully placed them in the pan. The cake was fresh and moist.

As hard as Hal tried, there was no fitting this cake together like a puzzle. She was just lucky to make the pan look full. The cake's top was uneven, but she couldn't do a thing about that. It was minus smeared icing, raisins and small crumbs that stuck to the floor. She picked some of the raisins out of the mess on the floor and sprinkled them on top the chunks in the pan. When she heard Emma coming, she snatched the pan off the floor and headed for the door.

"What's taking you so long?" Emma said as she met Hal in the doorway. "I thought I heard a noise." She stared at the mess in the cake pan then grimaced. Looking bewildered, she whispered, "What happened to my raisin spice cake?"

"I'm so sorry. The pan slipped out of my hands and fell on the floor." Hal paused, biting her lower lip. "Oh, Emma, the cake landed upside down. I picked the pieces up the best I could. I know it looks terrible. What are we going to do?"

"We have no choice. I invited the bishop's wife to have cake. We will serve the cake buried under lots of canned peaches to hide it." Emma snatched the pan out of Hal's hands and whispered, "It is a gute thing for you I mopped the floor this morning. Call Jane and my brothers into the kitchen. Wait! First, wash your hands."

Hal headed for the washpan to get rid of the moist crumbs and icing that had adhered to her fingers. Good thing Emma noticed. All Jane needed was one look at her messy hands. That would have been a dead give away. Emma, tired of waiting on her to wash up, called Jane and the boys to the table. Meekly, Hal sat down across from Jane.

As she took the blue, plastic bowl Emma handed her, Jane asked, "Nurse Hal, how do you like the clinic?"

"I like it very much. We aren't as busy as I would like yet, but I hope that day will come. After we eat if you have time, I can show you the clinic," Hal said. If she kept Jane talking until she ate the cake, the woman might not realize what kind of a mess she was eating.

"I would like that. Will you be able to deliver babies here?"

Taken back by the question, Hal said slowly, "I didn't give that any thought, but I don't know why not if that is a need. I thought Plain women had their babies at home or at the hospital."

"They do, but to be at a clinic this close to home with a nurse and know that they would soon be able to take the baby home will be a comfort," Jane said, taking a bite of peaches and cake.

Emma set a bowl in front of Hal.

Still thinking about another exciting way the clinic would be useful to the Amish, Hal picked up her spoon. "As long as there is no complications, I wouldn't mind birthings. If there is something wrong the women would have to go to the hospital so a doctor could help with labor," Hal said with a suspicious feeling. As she took a bite of cake, it ran through her mind that Elton's wife was sure asking a lot of questions.

"I understand," Jane said. "Emma, we need to get Nurse Hal acquainted with the community. How about we have a quilting bee at my house in a few days?" She listed the women she intended to invite including Stella Strutt.

Hal tensed at the whole idea.

"That sounds like fun," said Emma, frowning at Hal's reaction then smiling at Jane.

A quilting bee didn't sound the least bit fun to Hal. Sitting in a group of women she wanted to like her with Stella

Strutt putting her down and giving her the evil eye wasn't going to be helpful. She was just learning to sew. Stella was always ready to find fault with her. She'd be sure to point out Hal couldn't make stitches as fine as the other women. Hal had to think up an excuse to get out the quilting bee. That's all there was to it.

"The cake and peaches are very gute," Jane said to Emma.

Noah agreed, smacking his lips, "Very gute."

With his mouth full, Daniel garbled, "I like it, too."

"Thank you," Emma said. "Daniel, do not talk with your mouth full."

Elton appeared in the doorway. "What is going on in here?"

John was behind him. "Did I hear Jane mention cake and peaches?"

"A fresh raisin spice cake. Sit down and have some with us," Emma invited.

Elton entwined his chubby, red fingers and stretched his hairy plump arms out on the table. "I like your cakes, Emma. Make mine a big piece."

Emma blushed.

On edge while she waited for Elton to tell her his real reason for this visit, Hal scooped up a heaping spoonful of cake with a peach on top, but she was too nervous to eat. She left her spoon resting in the bowl. Almost too worried to breathe, she looked from Elton to John. When was Elton going to tell her what was wrong? Before he ate his cake or after? If that wasn't enough to worry about, now she had to wait to see if the men noticed anything wrong with the cake?

Hal started to relax about the time Elton swallowed the last bite of cake. So far, he had been friendly as long as he was preoccupied with eating. He looked at the empty saucer as he licked his spoon clean. Suddenly, Elton's head shot up. He said sharply, "Emma, there was something wrong with this cake!"

Emma's face flushed as her voice rose, "What?"

With a gasp, Hal dropped her shaky hand onto the table

111

to brace herself for what Elton was going to say. Her hand connected forcefully with her spoon handle. The end of the loaded spoon shot up out of the saucer, propelling the cake chunk into John's hair. The peach took a separate flight path and landed on Elton's bald spot.

Elton and John's eyes met in surprise before their narrowed eyes focused on Hal. John gave her a very disapproving look as he said to Elton, "Have you changed your mind about the difference between the child and the storm?"

"I am thinking on it," Elton said, looking flustered.

Hal slid down in her chair.

The boys grinned from ear to ear. Noah whispered in Hal's ear. "You have gute aim."

"I didn't do that on purpose," hissed Hal, eying Elton with a pleading look for forgiveness.

Rising quickly, Jane picked the peach off Elton's head and dropped the slice in his empty bowl. "It is just a little peach slice, Elton," she said as if that made some difference in the degree of Hal's assault.

Emma shot out of her chair and stood over her father. She grabbed his bowl and spoon. With a few quick swoops, she had most of the splattered mess off John's hair. Hal was too mortified to speak or react. Once again when she had to make a good impression, she was an Amish threat to the Lapp family. This time her assault was on the bishop. She didn't know how things could get much worse than that. Biting her lower lip, she helplessly watched Emma and Jane fuss over the men.

It didn't help to look at Noah and Daniel. They were having too good a time. Hal had to set this right. Not only for her good standing in the bishop's eyes. She couldn't let the boys think it was all right to play this kind of practical joke on company. The boys putting duck eggs under Emma's hen didn't begin to stack up with what she just did to the bishop and their father. What kind of a motherly example was she showing these boys anyway?

After Jane and Emma sat down, everyone looked wordlessly at Hal. She cleared her throat and found a voice unfamiliar to her, croaky as a frog. "I am so sorry. I don't know what made me so careless. Truly, I'm very, very sorry, Elton and John."

Emma came to her rescue, putting her arm around Hal. "Hallie is tired. She must have dozed off. Her hand slipped. What she needs is a gute night's rest."

John said dryly, "It is time I washed my hair anyway." As if that ended the matter, John turned to Elton. "Before Hal's piece of cake rained down on us, what was it you were going to say about the cake?"

Hal darted a hopeless look at Emma. John had no idea how not over this subject was if the bishop had noticed the scrambled mess he just ate.

Elton cleared his throat. He eyed Hal's hand as if he feared it might go off again and said in a subdued voice, "Only that my piece was so gute it was not big enough."

Hal went limp.

Emma asked meekly, "Would you care for another piece, Elton?"

"That would not do," said Jane, standing up. "More cake would spoil his supper."

Hal felt a tightness in her chest when Emma asked, "Will you stay for supper?"

"Thank you, but we should go home. We will stay another time," Jane said. As the Lapp family gathered to follow the Bontragers out on the porch, Jane gave Hal a warm smile and took her hand. "Do not forget to come with Emma to the quilting bee next week."

"Okay, thank you for asking me," Hal said halfheartedly. No way would she forget about the quilting bee. She'd be too busy worrying how to get out of it.

While waiting for supper, John sat down in his rocker to read his bible. As Hal and Emma started back to the kitchen, he asked, "What was that Jane said about a quilting bee?"

"Daed, Jane has asked Hallie and me to come to her house one afternoon next week for a bee," Emma said with excitement in her voice.

"Are you too busy to go?" John had a sober expression Hal didn't like seeing. Was he trying to vaguely warn Emma she shouldn't take Hal out in public after what she did to him and Elton?

"I can make time. Hallie needs to meet other Plain people," insisted Emma.

"Is Stella Strutt going to be there?" Something in the sound of his voice bothered Hal even more when he said that disagreeable woman's name.

Emma said offhandedly, "Jah."

Hal had to prove to John that she could get along with his friends. She was willing to bet Stella didn't have friends, but she'd have learn to turn the other cheek around Stella. "Don't worry, John. I promise to get along with Stella." In an after thought she added under her breath, "In a crowd."

John grimaced as he slowly shook his head.

"If you're worried about me. I promise not to do anything at all embarrassing at Jane's house in front of the other women," Hal declared.

"I'm not worried as long as Jane does not serve you cake," John said with a quiver at the corners of his mouth. He sighed. "I just thought you might not want to go if you knew Stella Strutt was invited."

Emma assured him, "Of course, Hallie knew. She wants to go. Jane says it will be a gute way for her to meet other women. It will be gute for the clinic if Plain people get to know Hallie."

John threw up his hands in surrender. With a solemn look of defeat on his face, he opened his bible.

After supper, Hal waited for John to bring up the fact that they should have that serious talk he promised, but he seemed to be distracted. She didn't dare ask why. Whatever the bishop told John was worrying him more than his problem with her. She'd just have to wait for him to decide to confide in her. Anger built up in her. That time might never come. For sure, it didn't look like it was going to happen tonight. Maybe that was just as well since she hadn't decided if she wanted to marry

114

him if it meant giving in to his "boss" law.

Whatever Elton said to John was worrying him too much to be bothered with her. Right this minute, she didn't think she could stand knowing what was that terrible. Not with the way she was feeling. She didn't need the bishop's negative attitude heaped onto her own problems. There was only one good thing she could think about. If John waited long enough to have their talk, he might forget to bring up how mad he was about her table manners.

Chapter 11

When Hal walked into the kitchen on Sunday morning, Emma flitted from the work counter to the cookstove, humming. She stopped long enough to pour Hal a cup of coffee, motioned toward a chair and continued her work. An unusual amount of pots clustered on the stove, crowding each other for room. Emma took the lid off one and then another. Some she stirred and others she checked.

"Looks like you're fixing a feast. Is there a reason?" Hal asked before she took a sip from her cup.

Emma, in the middle of taste sampling, didn't have a chance to answer. Daniel burst into the kitchen. "They're here!"

"Who's here?" Hal asked. She didn't need an answer to that question, either. She looked over Daniel's head at Roseanna Miller. As pretty as ever, Roseanna, dressed in her black mourning clothes, didn't look pale or dull eyed like a woman who had recently lost her husband. The wind, during the buggy ride, had buffed the young woman's cheeks with a rose blush. Her eyes sparkled with a new zest for life. Hal felt jealousy creeping up on her. Was Roseanna so cheerful because she was glad to see John?

Emma dried her hands on her apron and rushed to give Roseanna a hug. "Welcome. Join Hallie and me. I am so glad you could come."

"It was gute of you to invite my family and Samuel," said Roseanna, blushing shyly.

"Samuel Nisley came with you?" Came out of Hal's surprised mouth before she could stop herself.

"Jah, Samuel brought us," Roseanna continued. "He is outside with John, sitting on the porch. No telling where my two children are by now. Once they get with Noah and Daniel, the four of them scatter like quail." She laughed at the thought.

"Roseanna, would you like to have a cup of tea or coffee?" Emma asked.

Much to Hal's disapproval, Roseanna made herself right at home. "No. Can I help with dinner, Emma?"

"You can set the table. The food will be ready soon," Emma told her, looking in another pot.

Sure. I'm sitting here like the lazy hen Stella Strutt once called me. Emma could have asked me to help her but instead she lets Roseanna, Hal complained inwardly.

Roseanna looked from Emma to Hal with a cheerful smile. "It is so gute to see you both again."

Emma gave her a hug. "It is so gute you came for dinner."

The two women had known each other longer than Hal knew Emma. They liked each other and got along so well. Hal felt her eyes turning green as they darted an imaginary emerald laser beam at Roseanna.

"It feels gute to visit. It has been a long time since I felt like leaving home. I am grateful to Samuel for driving us here and for your invitation," Rosanna said sincerely to Emma.

Emma darted a glance at Hal. Just long enough to catch the long, hard stare Hal focused on her. Emma deliberately turned her back. This whole thing smelled like a conspiracy. This was Emma's idea to throw her and Roseanna together in the same room.

"It has been hard to feel happy for such a long time since Emil went and kicked the bucket." Roseanna swiped at a tear in the corner of her eye with her finger. "But that is getting

117

better," she said softly as she set the last plate on the table.

Why wouldn't things get better for her if she was set on marrying John Lapp, Hal thought.

Emma touched Roseanna's arm. "I am glad to hear you say that."

Roseanna patted her hand. "Jah, I am blessed in many ways, and I should remember that."

Emma turned to Hal with a smile that would melt butter. "You should show Roseanna our clinic while I am watching the food cook." She helped Hal up and took both women by the arm. She marched them toward the door as she said to Roseanna, "We are very proud of it."

"Jah, I would like to see the clinic," Roseanna said with curious enthusiasm.

Hal felt like a truck named Emma had just flattened her. As she left the kitchen with Roseanna, she heard Emma humming softly at the stove. Hal always took for granted that the kitchen was Emma's domain, but now it looked like she had branched out.

Roseanna walked around the clinic taking in everything. Hal leaned against the wall with her hands behind her back. Roseanna looked at the cupboards, in the cupboards and patted the quilt on the bed. "I remember this quilt. We quilted it at Linda Yoder's house." Finally, she sat down at the table. "Join me, Nurse Hal."

Hal sat down across from her.

Roseanna looked out the window. "I can see Emma's garden from here."

"Yes, Emma and I are working on the garden. I've found out gardens are quite an undertaking. Emma sure takes hers seriously," Hal said, eying the widow.

Something in Hal's tone made Roseanna study her. Not long, but enough to make Hal nervous. "Yes, growing food is important to keep us from going hungry. But what you do is important and special, too. Anyone can grow a garden, but not everyone can be a nurse like you. One that is so gute at helping people in need as you are." Roseanna gave her a sad smile. "I'll never forget how hard you tried to save Emil." She laid her hand on Hal's.

With the gentle warmth of Roseanna's hand touching hers, Hal felt her jealousy melt away. She said earnestly, "I just wish I could have been successful."

Looking out the window but not really seeing what was there anymore, Roseanna said softly, "Many times, I have wished the same thing. I miss my husband. Sometimes, the worries that used to be shared with Emil are almost beyond my ability to endure. I struggle to hang onto the farm for my son to take over when he is grown. Without the milk check, we could not manage. We would have no way to pay the land taxes. Even if we succeed at keeping our farm, sadness overwhelms me when I look at my children. I realize they will grow up without their father."

So are you telling me you need John more than I do? Hal thought. Out loud she said, "It's hard to get on top of such feelings, isn't it?"

"Jah. I am a hard worker. Though I can do much of what Emil did, working the land and milking the cows, I have always taken care of the house, raised the children, fed the family, gardened. I can still keep us fed if I garden, but to plow, plant, harvest crops and milk cows twice a day plus all the household duties is more than I can handle," Roseanna said honestly.

"So you need John's help, milking the cows," suggested Hal. She steeled herself for Roseanna to tell her John was the answer to all the Miller family's prayers. So Hal should just give up hope of ever becoming a part of the Lapp family.

Roseanna continued. "And Elton Bontrager planting the crops. It felt like Samuel was a Godsend when he showed up to take over. John needed a break to tend to his farming and to be with ----." Raising her eyebrows, she paused, studied Hal's face then continued, "with his family."

Hal was caught off guard. Somehow, Roseanna must know how fond John was of her. How? Happy as a meadowlark perched on top of the wood cookstove, Emma's humming grew louder. Of course. It was Emma who told her.

The woman rushed on, "I am so grateful for all my neighbors. I appreciate what they have done for my family in Emil's memory. May God reward them for helping me in my time of need."

"Maybe I simplify life too much, but when I'm having a bad time, I just imagine myself in a better place in the future where I'll be happy again. It works for me," Hal said, softening toward Roseanna because of her troubles. It was easier now to feel compassion for the woman. Much easier now that she knew Roseanna realized there was no hope of John marrying her.

"For me, it helped when I thought of a bible verse. I sought the Lord, and He answered me, and delivered me from my fears. I had a talk with myself. I told myself to stop wallowing in self-pity. I have my children. They need me. I must find a way to go on." Roseanna cocked her ear toward the porch, listening to Samuel chuckle at something John said. Her eyes glowed as she smiled at Hal. "These days it is easier to believe I am delivered from my fears. A dark cloud will often have a silver lining." She looked out the window and said with meaning, "I have found my silver lining. Is it not strange how life turns out?"

"I understand, and I agree," Hal said, trying to digest the fact that Roseanna was fond of Samuel. A feeling as light as floating feather lifted a great weight from inside her. It was easy for her to say goodbye to Mr. Jealousy now that Roseanna and she shared secrets.

"Now tell me, are you coming to the quilting bee at Jane Bontrager's?" Roseanna asked.

"I've been invited," Hal hedged. "Are you going?"

"Jah, you should come. It will be fun," Roseanna said.

Hal glanced toward the porch and wrinkled her nose. "That's what Emma said, but John didn't seem so enthusiastic about my going."

"Why not?"

"I'm not sure. Sometimes, the most embarrassing things

happen when I'm around. Perhaps, John is afraid about what his friends will think of me," suggested Hal.

Roseanna gave her a very sympathetic look. "I can not imagine anyone worrying about you not getting along well. The women in the Plain community will love you once they get to know you. Please come."

"There is one problem that could prove John right. I don't know how to sew," Hal confessed.

"Plain women are not born with the talent for sewing. They learn it with practice. You can, too," Roseanna said as if she had confidence in Hal.

"Emma is trying to teach me. We'll see," Hal said, still being noncommittal. "Let's go see if we can help Emma. More than likely she is about ready to have us sit down to eat."

Roseanna laughed. "Emma, is such a daerrich szwanger."

After the Miller family and Samuel left, Emma said to Hal, "Sit down at the table and talk to me. I am curious to know what Roseanna thought of the clinic."

Picking at a bread crumb Emma missed when she wiped the table, Hal said, "She was impressed. She said your father was very smart to have thought of such a handy thing for Plain people." Hal darted a look at Emma.

The girl gave her a searching look. Hal could read her like a book. Emma thought a compliment from Roseanna about her father would still bother her. As if anything nice said about John by Roseanna was a sign of her affection for him. True Hal had thought that up until today, but she was relieved to be able to put that behind her.

"Tell me, did you invite Roseanna for dinner for a reason? Maybe so I'd get to know her better?" Hal asked curiously.

Chapter 12

Emma knew she was busted. She gave Hal a slow nod yes.

"Well, don't worry about your sneaky plan. It worked," Hal said with a wide grin.

"What worked, Hallie?" Emma asked hopefully.

"Roseanna is a sweet person. I like her. She said it was a good idea John had when he talked me into running the clinic. She was glad that I'm here to help Plain people," Hal admitted. "She seemed so genuinely pleased to see me again and talk to me. How could I not like her?"

"Gute," Emma said with a sigh of relief.

"What did she mean when she said you were day rich wanger?"

"What? Ach, daerrich szwanger. She was telling you I do things in a hurry," Emma said smiling.

"Roseanna's right. That you do. I'd say that daerrich szwanger applies to the tasks you take on other than your household duties." Hal paused when Emma gave her a disheartening look. "I got the impression she knew your father is romantically involved with me."

Shrugging her shoulders, Emma ducked her head to hide the glow in her eyes. "I think it is just that Roseanna is very observant. Sometimes just looking at you and Daed together, how you feel about each other is easy to see. Otherwise, I am sure I can not say how Roseanna came by that idea."

"Or won't," whispered Hal as Noah and Daniel came in the kitchen for a drink of water.

To change the subject, Emma said to Hal, "Time to gather eggs." She sighed. "I think of Zacchaeus every time I go to the hen house. I wonder where he got off to." With meaning, she said for her brothers benefit, "Some day I hope those who know what happened to my rooster feel guilty enough to tell me. They should be very sorry for taking my rooster from me."

Noah gave Hal a wounded look over the top of the dipper as he took a sip.

Daniel turned his back to the table so he didn't have to face Hal and Emma when he took the dipper from his brother.

Hal held her breath as she waited. True to their word, neither boy spoke up. Quietly, they went back outside to do their chores.

After supper that evening, Emma and Hal just about had the kitchen tidied when Hal peered in the living room. With his head leaned back on his rocker, John dozed as usual. His Bible had slipped out of his hands and lay on the edge of his lap. In the glow of the kerosene lamp, the boys played scrabble at the table.

"Emma, I think I'm going to sit on the porch for awhile. I need some fresh air," Hal said dully.

As she walked by the boys, Noah asked, "Want to play a game with us?"

"We will play in English," Daniel said, trying to tempt her.

"That's kind of you. Actually, it'd do me good to play in Dutch so I learn the language, but I think I will pass tonight. I'm going to sit on the porch for awhile and watch the moon come up." She started for the door.

"Ask her," Daniel hissed at Noah.

Hal stopped and came back. "Ask me what?"

123

The boys glanced over to see if their father was still asleep.

"We wondered if you would ask Daed to get us another dog?" Noah whispered.

"I didn't think you ever wanted another one," said Hal.

"We did not at first, but now we miss having a dog to play with," Daniel shared.

"I see. Why don't you ask your father?"

"We did mention it, but he did not seem too interested," Noah said.

"If you ask him maybe he will get us a dog for you," Daniel said, giving her his wide doe eyed look.

"For me?" Hal shook her head and said truthfully, "I'm not so sure your father is willing to listen to me about anything, but if I get a chance to bring it up, I'll see what I can do."

"Danki," Daniel said, squeezing her hand. "One more thing. We want to know if you will teach us that spoon trick."

"The spoon trick? Oh no! No, I won't. That was an accident. I'm in a lot of trouble with the bishop and your father because of that. Don't ever try doing it on anyone or you will get me in more trouble, because your father knows you learned it from me," Hal hissed. "Promise me."

"We promise," Noah said.

Daniel concentrated on pushing a scrabble tile around in a circle.

Hal took Daniel by the chin and made him look up at her. "Daniel, promise."

"All right, I promise. I still think it was a gute trick," he said, smiling at her.

As Hal sat down on the edge of the porch, her worries piled up on her. Too many awful things going wrong in her life to think about in front of the others. What had happened lately kept her feelings all shook up. She folded her arms across her legs and laid her face down. Feeling physically drained, she knew she should go back to her apartment before John woke up. She wasn't fit company for anyone. Not even herself.

She closed her eyes to shut out the image of John,

124

glaring at her. If they did have a talk, she could imagine him saying he'd changed his mind about marrying her. He didn't want to spend the rest of his days with a English red head that couldn't seem to do anything right. That would certainly keep her from having to make the decision about marrying him.

After a while, the front door squeaked opened. Hal heard the soft thud of footsteps on the porch floor boards. She was nudged by someone sitting beside her and felt a tentative touch on her shoulder.

"Thought you were going to watch the moon come up?"

"Decided I didn't want to," Hal mumbled.

"I am supposed to tell you we just had a family meeting," John stated.

His body felt warm and strong against Hal. That was no comfort to her now. His family had excluded her from their family meeting. That didn't bode well for her future.

"Without me," she said flatly, eying a crack in the wooden step between her feet.

"It was Emma's idea. She did not want me to ask you to be there this time. The meeting was about you. Emma says you have not looked pretty gute for a long time. She said it was time I should notice. My daughter is right. You do not look gute," John said with conviction.

"Thanks a lot," sniffed Hal, huffily.

"You are welcome." After a pause, John cleared his throat. "Emma reminded me I was going to have a talk with you before the Bontragers came to visit. My daughter is one determined young woman when she wants something done. This talk between us is long overdue, but I put it off on purpose. I did not want to face your decision about marrying me. I have feared you might say no.

Emma says something is wrong. I am to find out what is bothering you. First, you need to hear me out. We do need to sort out what is wrong before we can go on together with our lives." He amended, "If we are going to be together. I have been thinking about what I need to say. It hurts me that you do not trust me to help a woman in need. Are you ever going to accept that there is not and will never be anything between me and Roseanna Miller? You are making yourself miserable for nothing."

In John's voice, she heard a quiet frustration on the verge of anger. He was to the point that he had waited long enough for her to come to her senses. Hal slowly brought her head up. In a strained voice, she said, "That's not it anymore. Really it's not"

John put his hands on her shoulders and twisted her around so their eyes met. "Are you sure? Emma says you told her this afternoon you like Roseanna. You do not act like this is the way you feel."

Casting aside her pride, Hal swallowed hard. "I do like Roseanna. I admit I had been jealous. For that I am really sorry. I suppose jealousy is an English fault that Amish never have," Hal accused, feeling judgmental.

"Do not believe that only English suffer from such faults. Plain people might try harder to overcome harmful emotions. I am at the end of my rope with you. I do not know what else I can say to make you believe that it is you I love," John said desperately.

Hal wiggled out of his grasp and put her head back down in her arms. "I've always believed that you love me. It's just that I kept comparing me to Roseanna. If I was a smart, good-looking Amish man like you which woman would I choose? Me or a woman who is young, beautiful and very dignified. She's already Amish. Roseanna knows the customs. Plain people accept her already. She would never do anything to embarrass you in front of your friends and family. She not only has poise but a graceful calm about her." Hal recited the list of Roseanna's attributes just like she had in her head a million times.

John relaxed against the porch post and rubbed his chin. "Danki for pointing out all of Roseanna's gute qualities to me. She is really all of that?"

Hal raised her head to finish her point. "And much

more than I'll never be. She owns a farm. Best of all, she can cook. She says you really like her doughnuts. I'll never be able to make doughnuts. Choosing between the two of us is like ---- like eating a sweet, yellow delicious and a rotten, sour apple."

The corners of John's mouth twitched. "Strange that I have never thought of you as rotten, sour or an apple. You are bright and full of life. Sometimes a little too spunky, but usually a pleasure to be with. Until lately that is," John amended wryly, looking down at his hands.

"If you mean that cake thing with the bishop. I said I'm sorry about that," Hal apologized.

"I am not talking about that. I am trying my best not to remember that moment," John said, rubbing the top of his head.

Hal turned to him and blurted out "I think Roseanna is interested in Samuel."

"Do you think? That would be gute, ain't so?" John watched her for a reaction.

Hal searched his face. "You wouldn't mind if Samuel proposed to Roseanna?"

"They would be a gute match," he agreed. "Besides it would stop those crazy thoughts in your head if Samuel wed Roseanna," he said honestly.

"John, I've already stopped those crazy thoughts. I am glad that Roseanna is happy again. I want her to be happy with Samuel," Hal declared. "I don't know what happened to me. When you weren't around, I missed you. The awful doubts about Roseanna and you kept popping into my head. What you just said was what I needed to hear straight out." She sighed and said with meaning, "It'd help if we could have these talks a little closer together from now on. I'm willing to adjust to most of your ways and understand".

"Gute. I agree we should talk out what bothers us just like we are doing now." Anxious, he asked, "Have you decided yet if you will marry me?"

John gave her a grave look, expecting a serious answer one way or the other. "I want to marry you. I'm just not sure I can be the kind of wife the Amish approve of or you for that matter," Hal said honestly.

"I was afraid you would see it that way," John said softly. "I think you will do just fine if you really want to be my wife. You have to decide what is most important to you, being English or Amish."

John had her on the spot. She had to make a commitment or go home. He expected an answer right now. She didn't like the thought of giving up her women's rights but the alternative was living alone and apart from the Lapp family. She didn't want her life to go back the way it was.

"I will marry you on your terms. The Amish way," Hal surrendered.

The look on John's face held relief and joy. "You had me worried. Do not ever do this to me again. I do not think my heart can stand it." He pulled her to him. "Now I know you really do love me. Would it help if I told you, I do not mind us the way we are? Maybe we could reach a compromise."

"Like what?" Hal said suspiciously.

John licked his lips and said meekly, "When we are out in a gathering could you try to let me be the head of the house?"

Hal giggled. "Try? Oh, John, I wouldn't have it any other way as long as I get a say when we're home," Hal declared.

"Gute, I like the sound of that," he said with relief in his voice.

Hal's eyes narrowed. "Why didn't you tell me about this compromise before?"

"I had to know you would marry me for me no matter what I ask of you," John said. "There is bound to be other problems that come up. Things that seem strange to you or difficult to accept. I did not want to find out later you do not love me enough to be with me."

"Now we know," Hal said, sounding down. John sure was right about other problems. She had one right here and now.

128

One look at Hal told John she still felt terrible. "But something else is wrong with you. If your worry is not about me being unfaithful or our marriage, what is it that makes you so sad? Emma thought you are afraid that you will not fit in as a Plain person. The Lapp family does not worry about that so you should not." He looked her directly in the eye, wanting her to feel his sincerity.

She tore her eyes from his face. She knew this talk would be difficult, but she didn't realize how hard until now. "It's true, I'm concerned that I might not be able to convince the bishop that I'll try hard to be Amish. I've had doubts about what I'm getting into with you. The future worries me a lot. Especially when I do stupid things like fling cake on the bishop and you. Elton may be wondering if he should turn me away before I harm someone. He probably thinks I'm crazy. I wouldn't blame him."

"He does not think you are crazy. You just try too pretty hard to please everyone," said John firmly. "Once you settle into the routine with us, everything you do will be second nature. You will not have to worry. Is that all that is bothering you? Forget about it if that is it."

"No, that isn't exactly all that's bothering me," Hal said in a whisper as she focused on the barnyard.

The Holstein bull rested his head on his pen fence, lifted up his nose and sniffed for airborne scents from the bawling cows. She thought about the day that bull knocked her out of his pen and broke her ribs. The squeal of pigs brought back to her their big escape which got her flattened by a sow. None of that was going to as painful as Emma being mad at her.

Chapter 13

John was persistent. He wasn't going to stop until Hal confessed. She pictured her fate when Emma found out she killed Zacchaeus. No belonging to this family, once that young lady called another family meeting which Hal wasn't invited to and voted her out of the family. All the happiness Hal had dreamed would be hers soon was coming quickly to a drop dead end. She had been within a hair's width of the happiness she wished for on that rainbow. That happiness was going to fly out the kitchen window once she confessed to Emma. She'd again be living alone in that small apartment in Wickenburg. Each day would wind up dull and lonely like the one before it. Hope and joy would just be distant wishful memories. It wouldn't matter that she loved John enough to give in to being a submissive wife.

Hal glanced wistfully at the sky above the barn. It was dusky dark and not a storm cloud in sight. No chance of a rainbow when she needed one to promise her the happiness she wished for. She wanted so desperately to have a hopeful sign to cling to. A rainbow to give her the courage to fight for what she wanted in life and protect her from feeling so lost and dismal. Instead, she was on her own and not so sure she could handle what was ahead of her. She was about to find out what twisted fateful havoc the truth would create in her life.

John cleared his throat and tried again. "Noah and Daniel said you are mourning the loss of Patches. They suggested that I get you a dog."

Hal gave John a weak smile. "They said that?"

"Jah."

With some humor in her voice, Hal said, "The boys are past mourning Patches. Would it surprise you to know they asked me to talk you into letting them have another dog? If that didn't work I'm to ask you to get me the dog."

"Ach, nah surprise that," he assured her. "Noah and Daniel have figured out that you have the power to persuade me in ways that they can not. You know that my sons love you like a mother." He licked his top lip. "One more thing you have failed to mention. It has been told to me that the boys call you Mama."

"Oh," Hal said in a small voice. "Honest, I told the boys we had to discuss it with you to make sure that was okay. Things have been so crazy lately, I just forgot."

"It would be nice to know what is going on with my family if you could remember to tell me important things from now on." Hal ducked her head, feeling chastened. John added, "My children are the happiest I have seen them in years. You are the reason for that. It gives me much joy to know you are going to be a part of this family. I want my children to think of you as a mother. If the boys feel comfortable calling you mama, that is all right with me."

"I'm so glad," Hal said with tears of relief in her eyes. "Who told you the boys call me Mama?"

"Elton mentioned it when he was here," John said offhandedly.

"Elton?" Hal asked, surprised. "How would Elton know such a thing? He hasn't been around since you built the clinic."

John rubbed his chin, picking his words carefully. "Elton had a visit from Stella Strutt. She heard the boys call you Mama the day Patches got run over."

"I might have known. Stella Strutt," Hal spit the words out like she was saying the name of a poisonous snake. "She

131

doesn't like me. I don't think she ever will."

"She will once she gets used to you. Right now you represent all that is English to her. You are too close to her home. She sees you as a threat, but that will change," John predicted.

Hal worried, "What did Elton think about what Stella told him?"

"He was most curious why I allowed an English person to be so close to my children. He is not dumb. He noticed the change in my family while he helped build the clinic. After Stella's visit, he gave that some thought. He remembered last winter Emma asked him about a friend of hers that was thinking about converting to Amish."

"Oh my," Hal gasped.

John said slowly, "He wanted me to spell out my intentions where you are concerned."

"What did you say?" She whispered.

John cocked an eye at her. "I told him I asked you to marry me."

Hal gripped his knee. "You did? What did he say?" Rushed out of her mouth.

"If you do not change your mind, you are to come talk to him when you are ready. He will decide after he meets with you."

Hal got a case of the jitters just thinking about meeting with the bishop. "It's too soon for that. I've much more to learn. My Dutch is not good yet. I don't know if I'm ever going to be able to understand all that I need to know about belief and customs," Hal excused but she added, "I am trying. Believe me, John. I am."

"Elton knows that. I told him so. I know that. Emma, Noah and Daniel know that so calm down," John reassured her.

Hal leaned her head to one side. "Did this talk happen when Elton asked you to look at his new horse?"

"Jah."

"I just knew it," Hal declared.

"How?"

"I was watching you out the window. You can't check a horse by looking the other way. At least John Wayne didn't do it that way," Hal said with conviction.

John looked really worried. His voice sounded edgy. "John Wayne? Is he another friend of yours like Bill?"

"Phil," she corrected. When she saw the worried look on his face, she almost laughed. John actually thought John Wayne was his competition. He had been right when he said the Amish had the same pangs of jealousy, but he was wrong when he said they fight it harder. She wanted to point that out, but she thought she better leave well enough alone. Maybe some other time when he wasn't so put out with her, she'd remind him of his reaction to John Wayne.

"Oh no," she assured him adamantly. "John Wayne was a western movie actor. He died about thirty years ago. When I watch his old movies on television, I've seen the way he checked a horse."

"Actor," John snorted. "Mind telling me how Mr. Wayne checks horses?"

"He opened the horse's mouth and looked at its teeth. He felt up and down the horse's legs and checked the bottom of its feet. John Wayne never checked a horse by standing around talking with his hands in his pockets like you did," Hal acknowledged.

"That might work for an English actor, but Amish do not have to check their horses that way. They are better judge of horse flesh than that. Now when looking at a woman to marry, that is another story," John said, giving her a tongue in cheek look.

"You're joking! Aren't you?

John put his hand on Hal's knee and slid it down her shin.

Pushing his hand away, she scooted over to the end of the step. "John Lapp, you are not going to treat me like a horse. You will just have to take my word for it I am sound of limb, and I have all my teeth."

"It is not your teeth or the bottom of your feet that I am

133

interested in," John said, grinning.

Hal bristled. "In that case, no reason not to give me the same treatment as you would a horse. Eying should be enough to make your decision. No feeling needed."

John exploded with laughter. He doubled over unable to control himself until he had to wipe tears from his cheeks. When he straightened up, Hal was looking off into space, wearing the same hang-dog look. Nothing had changed for her He held his arms out. "Hal, come here." She slid to him and let him hold her in his strong, warm arms. John put his cheek down in her fuzzy, copper red hair. "Mind telling me what is worrying you. You are the one that said we have to start telling each other what is bothering us. Did we not cover everything yet?"

"No," she said, her voice cracking. "We haven't covered the worse of it. Not at all. Not by a long shot." She burst into a flood of tears.

"Calm down. You must tell me now before this worry really does make you sick," demanded John in exasperation.

Hal took a deep breath. She had to stop the tears if she intended to confess. Right then she felt all color drain from her face. Her stomach churned just anticipating John's bad reaction. If she dreaded his reaction, think how much worse it would be when she had to face Emma.

She sniffled, "Give me your hanky."

"My schnopp-dooch?"

"Yes, your whatever you call it." She blew her nose in John's blue work hanky. That gave her a moment to find her voice while she dabbed her eyes. "All right, but I'm warning you right now, you're not going to like knowing. I did something bad. Real bad. I hate it. There's no undoing it. I've known all along I should be honest enough to confess, but I'm afraid that Emma will never forgive me."

"It is something to do with Emma that brought this worry on? Not me?" John asked in relief.

"Don't sound as if you're off the hook, Mister! You know Emma has a big say in what happens around here. You

134

might not like what she has to say about me when she knows. She might tell you to make me leave and not come back," warned Hal.

"Just tell me what is wrong." He took her by the shoulders and shook her gently. "I will decide who stays in my family."

Hal gave him a hard look. This must be the voice she was going to hear when he thought he was the boss. "I've been afraid to say anything, but I hate it that Emma is giving the boys a hard time about Zacchaeus disappearing. She blames Noah and Daniel. I feel sick at my stomach every time her pet rooster's name comes up."

"Emma will get another rooster. You are making yourself sick over a missing rooster?" John asked incredulously, trying to digest what she told him.

"Yes. You need to know the boys didn't hurt that rooster," defended Hal.

"I did not think they did. But are you telling me Noah and Daniel do know what happened to the rooster and did not tell us?" John looked grim.

Hal nodded. "Don't be mad at the boys. They're keeping quiet to protect me from getting in trouble with Emma. I felt so guilty I had to tell someone. When I helped the boys milk one night, what I did just came out."

"What did you do?" John sounded exasperated.

"I killed Emily's rooster, Zacchaeus," Hal moaned.

"You could not do such a thing."

Hal shook her head up and down as she assured him, "Oh, but I did."

John hugged her tight. His voice sounded gentle and warm, but she heard a touch of that irritating humor of his coming though. "Tell me what happened. I will decide how terrible you are."

She wrenched free. "If you are going to laugh at me I won't tell you. This is too horrible to laugh about. I will just go back to my apartment and cry myself to sleep."

John bit his lower lip and took a deep breath. When he

135

got hold of himself, his chocolate eyes held an over-abundant amount of sadness. He could see how hard Hal was struggling with her confession. "I promise never to make fun of you for something that makes you feel this bad. I never want you to keep a problem to yourself again when you are this upset. Will you promise me that?"

"Oh, yes. I never want to feel this bad again," Hal said adamantly.

"Gute. Mind telling me now. Please! You are driving me crazy," John begged.

Hal shook her head disbelievingly. "I don't know how you can always be so understanding. On the other hand, you might not be once you know."

John looked perturbed. He demanded, "Hal, out with it."

"It happened the Sunday Emma fixed fried chicken for dinner. I went with the boys to get two fryers. Noah caught two roosters in the hen house. He gave one to Daniel and the other to me. Daniel ran around back to wait for Noah to get the hatchet. I was following Daniel when my rooster acted up. He pecked me on the hand. It surprised me and sort of hurt. I dropped him, and he ran off. Another rooster came right up to me. I thought he was mean. That he had the idea to flog me. I reached down and managed to grab him by the tail. When Noah came back, I didn't want to tell him I lost the rooster he caught for me. I handed him the one I caught without telling him what I did. Noah cut Zacchaeus's head off. Oh if only I had it to do over again. I'd let Noah catch another fryer instead of doing it myself," she wailed.

"Did you know that the rooster you caught was Emma's pet?"

Hal shook her head hard enough to send her fuzzy hair flying. "No. I'd never do such a thing to Emma's pet on purpose. I didn't know I'd killed him until Emma asked the boys if they might have caught her rooster for that Sunday dinner. It was then that I realized what I did."

John stroked her head. "This was an accident. Emma

136

will understand and forgive you."

"I don't know why she would. She's already upset over Patches dying. Now to find out I'm the one that killed her rooster may be more than she can bear. Not only that, she'll feel bad every time she remembers she ate him. It will come back to her when we have fried chicken for dinner. Forgiving me will be more than she can cope with when she looks at me and at her drumstick."

"You know Emma is stronger than that if you settle down and think about it. She will forgive you," John said adamantly. "Trust me on this. Plain people have a saying. One lie brings the next one with it. It is not gute to let what happened hang in the air between you and Emma. She is worried about you. She misunderstood what was wrong. Right now she is blaming me for the way you feel. She's pestering me to make things right with you. You are right about one thing. I do not like Emma upset with me, either. I felt helpless not knowing what was wrong with you.

You did not seem to want to tell me. I did not like it that you would not share what was bothering you. On top of that, you put the boys in bad with their sister. You should think about Noah and Daniel. As bad as they feel about Emma mistrusting them, they choose to keep silent because they love you."

"You're right. I've taken advantage of those poor, little boys, because they were so willing to protect me. This afternoon Emma gave them a hard time about the rooster again. I felt so sorry for them. They will grow tired of waiting for me to come to my senses and grow to dislike me," Hal said with a long sigh.

"I think it is that you are having trouble figuring out what someone Plain like Emma would do," John predicted.

"That worries me no end. That and the fact, I think I am a hopeless bother. Will I ever catch on to the way you think?"

"Jah, just give yourself time," John said sincerely.

"Do all Amish have such blind faith or is it just you?"

"I cannot speak for others. It's you I want to have faith

in," he said, giving her a tight squeeze.

"The English see things so different. I fear all the time that I'll do or say something that will upset someone around here beyond repair. I seem to have a knack for doing the wrong things. Now I need to repair the damage I've done because of the rooster if I can, don't I?" She asked.

"Jah," John said.

"Now that you know, could you tell Emma for me? I'll go home right now and wait for her to cool off," Hal planned.

"No, I am not going to say a word. This is something you have to do," John told her.

"Guess I better go tell Emma what happened, huh? Will you come with me?" Hal asked hopefully.

"You need to do that alone. I will not come with you," John said inflexibly.

"Why? Scared?"

"Jah, I am not dumb. I do not want to be close to Emma until I know how she is going to take this news. I am not very gute sure what she will say," he admitted. The corners of his mouth twitched.

"Coward!" Hal scolded. She stamped her foot and went into the house.

Noah and Daniel looked up from a game of checkers when Hal closed the door.

"What is wrong, Mama Hal?" Noah asked.

"You look sick," added Daniel.

"I feel sick. I'm going to tell your sister what I did to her rooster so she'll quit giving you a hard time. Want to come with me?"

"Not me," Daniel said. "I have had enough of Emma's mean looks."

"Me, too, but it is gute that you do this," said Noah. "I will be glad to soon be off the hook."

"I'm sorry that Emma has been upset with you. That was not a nice thing for me to do to you. I should have told her sooner." Hal glanced toward the kitchen door. "If it sounds like she is going to hurt me, I'll yell help. Will you come save me?"

138

Daniel giggled, "Emma, will not hurt you."

"But if she does, we will think about helping you. Nah promises," Noah said with a boyish grin so like his father's.

"Oh, you two are a big comfort." Hal braced herself, took a deep breath and walked into the kitchen.

Surprised, Emma looked up from her garden book. "I thought you went home."

"Your father told me about the meeting. We had that talk you wanted," Hal said.

"Gute. Did it help you?"

"Oh, yes. Now I understand he will inspect me like a horse before he marries me," sniffed Hal.

"What did he say to you?" Emma's voice was sharp.

"Oh, I shouldn't have said anything. I think he was joking. John told me I've worried you. For that I'm sorry. I need to tell ----."

Emma shot up from her chair and flitted to the cookstove so fast the strings on her prayer cap flew out behind her. She pulled the cast iron tea kettle to the front. "First listen to me. I tried my best to help make things better for you, Hallie, so you would not leave us. I do not want you to go." Wadding her apron tail in her hand, she picked up the hot lid. Looking into the kettle, she said, "I thought I could help by taking you to Roseanna's house. It might have worked if she had not said all those kind things about Daed." She dropped the lid noisily back into place.

She's really getting excitable. This isn't helping, Hal thought. "Emma, ----."

The girl wasn't listening. "I hoped inviting Roseanna and Samuel to dinner might help you feel better when you saw them together." Emma set the kettle down hard on the counter. The aluminum, long-handled dipper bounced up in the water pail and clattered back against the metal bucket. She snatched the hot lid off with her bare hand, fumbled with it and lost her grip. The lid rolled along the counter and fell with a bang to the floor.

Chairs scraped against the hardwood floor in the living

room. The boys were ready to come help or run the other direction. Hal glanced toward the kitchen door, wondering what they had decided to do. If they were coming, she hoped they would hurry up before Emma exploded.

Hal opened her mouth to speak, but she didn't get a chance.

"If you saw that Roseanna and Samuel liked each other, I hoped that would help the way you felt," Emma continued in a frenzy. She paused long enough to fill the kettle with water then picked up the lid. She slammed it on the kettle forcefully. "That did not work. Something still bothered you. I asked Daed to talk to you." She flashed to the stove.

Oh no, she's working herself up into a real tizzy, Hal worried.

"Did he do it? Jah, but all he did was upset you worse with what he said. I told him to try again. He did not until tonight after I reminded him again with a potholder upside the head," Emma said. "What did he do? Let you think he is going to treat you like livestock before you can be a member of this family." She set the tea kettle down hard enough on the stove water shot out of the spout. Little sputtering beads jumped across the hot surface.

Just listening to Emma, Hal wondered if the girl knew about the Amish commandment that the man in the family was boss in all things. The idea came to her, the compromise with John was going to be a cinch if she took her cue from Emma. John may talk big, but so far Emma wore the pants in the Lapp family. John just didn't seem to notice.

Hal had to stop Emma from chattering and calm her down. If she let Emma stew much longer, the girl wasn't ever going to forgive her. Hal rushed over to her. "Emma, please let me say something. Sit down and listen to me. Don't get mad at your father. It's bad enough that you're mad at the boys because of me."

"I am not mad at the boys. I am sorry, Hallie, for going on this way. Sit down and talk to me." Emma pointed to a chair and chose one herself.

140

Hal ignored the invitation to sit and persisted, "Yes, you are mad at your brothers. Because of your pet rooster."

"Achh that. What has that to do with you, Hallie?" Emma asked, puzzled.

"You're not going to like what I have to tell you, but I have to say it." Hal braced herself against the counter and folded her arms across her chest. She wasn't a complete dummy. She wasn't about to sit down. All too quick, she might need to propel herself away and out of the kitchen. " I killed your rooster."

"Oh! That is not funny. You would not do such a thing." Emma didn't believe her.

Hal shook her head up and down. "I'm not trying to be funny. Believe me, I haven't felt like laughing for days. I did kill him. I did not kill your rooster on purpose, but I did it."

Emma propped her elbows on the table and rested her hands under her chin. She looked at Hal sideways. "How?"

Steepling her fingers together, Hal gripped her hands tight at her waist and told the whole story just as she had told it to John. Her voice was so low Emma had to lean closer to hear. Finally, Hal concluded with, "There you have the whole dreadful nightmare. I killed Zacchaeus, and you ate him."

Emma had an incredulous look on her face. "This is what has been bothering you? I thought it was Roseanna or something Daed did."

"You're right on both those counts, but I came to my senses where Roseanna and your father is concerned. Killing your rooster has been bothering me a lot longer. Can you ever forgive me for doing such an awful thing?" Hal asked, looking miserable.

"You said you would not harm my pet rooster on purpose. I believe you. I am relieved to know what happened so I can quit pestering my brothers about it. I will say I forgive you if that will make you feel better. I want you to feel better. I am very glad you and Daed made up. You have to know I so worried this family was going to lose you. I love you more than any old rooster." Emma gave her a heartwarming smile.

"Thank you," Hal said bursting into tears. For days, she'd had a tight feeling in her chest like an over-wound clock. So tight a pressure that she felt as if her chest might split open from the pain. That had gone away now just as fast as it came. "I feel so much better now that I've confessed."

"Gute. There is no pillow as soft as a clear conscience. Now you will be glad to know you will not be thought of in the same way Zacchaeus was in the Bible," said Emma, smiling.

"How was that?"

"He was a very dishonest man."

It was then that Hal realized the walls behind the kitchen doorway had ears. Noah whispered something to do with Roseanna Miller. Daniel wondered why Nurse Hal would be mad at their father. All the while, John, making hissing sounds, did his best to silence their voices.

"Emma, do you suppose we could start over from scratch with a clean slate?" Hal asked.

"Ach, Hallie, no need to start over." Emma giggled as she came around the table. "But some day soon we need to have a discussion about the animals we raise on this farm. You need to understand what happens to them so you do not feel bad about killing a chicken." She gave Hal a hug.

"I grew up on a farm. I'm well aware farm animals are income and food. I just wasn't sure how the Amish felt about pets," Hal explained.

"A pet cannot replace a human in my affections. Remember that," Emma said seriously.

"Thank you for being so understanding," Hal said, smiling with tears of relief bubbling out of her eyes. She wiped her eyes with John's hanky and nodded toward the door. Putting a finger to her lips, she whispered, "Do you think we should go get the guys away from the wall before they come down with irreversible flatearitis?"

"Is that a medical term?"

"No, I just made it up. That, my dear Emma, is a symptom of eavesdropping in my medical terminology."

When Hal and Emma pounced out of the kitchen, Noah

and Daniel were on one side the door, flattened against the wall. John leaned on the other side, his legs crossed at the ankles.

"What's going on in here?" Hal asked casually.

"Not much," Daniel said. He fiddled with his straw hat on the wall peg. "I am straightening my hat."

"I am looking for something. I thought I left it in my jacket," Noah said, going through the pockets.

"How about you, Daed?" Emma asked.

Her father shrugged his shoulders. "Just resting."

"I'm going back to town now. John, since you are all rested up, would you like to walk me to my car?" Hal asked.

"Jah," he said with a lopsided grin.

When they reached her car, Hal turned and smiled at him. "Good night, Mr. Lapp."

She reached for the door handle. John put his hand over hers and brushed her lips with a light kiss. "I love you, Hal. Always remember that."

"I intend to from now on," she replied.

Chapter 14

The next day, Hal rushed to get from one senior citizen client to another. She'd had many a sleepless night lately, but today she had a clear conscious. For the first night in ages, she slept so sound she woke up late and had been behind all morning.

Too late, she arrived at Mrs. Johnson's apartment after the lady called Barb Sloan. She handed the phone to Hal. Hal explained she was just a little behind and Barb hung up. Finally a little after lunchtime, Hal finished her rounds.

She couldn't wait to get to the farm. As she stopped, she spotted the horse and buggy parked by the barn. John must be going somewhere. Maybe she would catch him before he left. She rushed up the porch steps. The clinic door opened. John was waiting for her. He kissed her, stepped out on the porch and closed the door behind him.

He said, "I want you to go for a ride with me over to Luke Yoder's farm this afternoon. Visit his family. Is that all right?"

"Okay."

"Wait here. I will tell Emma to watch the clinic."

Their destination was about five miles away. An hour later, John turned into the Yoder driveway. Chickens scratched in the barnyard, clucking over finding a bunch of cinch bugs.

The Yoder dog yapped his company coming warning toward the house. He ran over to stand under the clothes flapping on the line. The dog turned his head with the sway of a blue shirt, eying it wistfully. Hal noted how neat Amish hang up wet clothes. Starting with small clothes and going to larger ones, the colors, green, blue, purple and pink, reminded Hal of a rainbow.

Luke came out of the house to greet them. "Get out and come in." The dog barked playfully. Luke looked at the clothes line just in time to see the dog lunge at a shirt sleeve. "No, Jonah. Stop that," he yelled. He turned toward the screen door and called, "Levi, come out here and get that dog before he eats another hole in one of my gute shirts."

Levi burst out of the house and rushed past John and Hal on the porch steps. John shook hands with Luke. By that time, two women, one dressed in a soft green dress and the other in black, came out of the house. Another boy and two small girls stood behind the women. Luke introduced his dark-haired wife, Linda. She had a quiet, unassuming air about her much like her husband.

When Luke introduced his children, they nodded and ducked their heads to watch their bare feet. "The boy is Mark, the taller girl is Jenny and the other is Rose." Pointing to the woman in black, he said, "This is my mother, Margaret Yoder."

Under her prayer cover, Margaret's dark brown hair was threaded with silver. When they shook hands, she gave Hal a warm smile that reached to her light brown eyes and made the wrinkles fan out at the corners.

The men sauntered off to sit under a shade tree. The children ran to catch up with Levi and the dog.

Linda said, "I'll fix us all a glass of tea."

"We have been curious about you. It is so nice to meet you after all we have heard," said Margaret, looking at Hal intently.

"Mama Margaret, while I fix the tea why not take Nurse Hal to see our garden. I will yell when I need help carrying the glasses," suggested Linda.

"I'd love to see your garden," Hal told her. "Emma is making a garden. She's teaching me how."

"Come this way. Our garden is down by the road." As they walked along, Margaret asked, "How is the clinic doing?"

"The clinic is fine, but I was hoping that it would be busier than it is. I haven't had a patient for days. I guess that it is a good thing if no one needs my help," Hal said, reminding herself that was what Emma would say.

"Perhaps. The clinic might take time. Sometimes, Plain people have trouble getting used to new ideas. You might find this to be true with the clinic," suggested Margaret

"You might say that about English people, too, if you were among them for awhile," suggested Hal.

"I did find that out many times," Margaret said with a slight smile. "You see for a long time I lived an English life."

Hal couldn't have been more surprised if Margaret had stepped on her toes. "Really? You're English?"

"No, I am Amish. I left the Amish ways behind when I was young. Married a successful lawyer and became English. My husband had money so I had all the English conveniences I wanted." Margaret clasped her hands behind her back and kept walking.

"How did you wind up here? Oh, if you don't mind me asking," Hal said.

"I do not mind. I want to tell you. John says you are having a hard time getting used to Amish ways. He thought it might help if I share my story with you." She stopped. "As long as we have come, for Linda, we best take a look at the garden."

"Your rows are neat just like Emma's. This is a very nice garden," Hal complimented.

"If only everything in our lives could be put into neat, orderly rows. Recht, Nurse Hal?" Margaret asked, smiling at her.

"Yes, but tell me how you became Amish again."

"I was not happy with a wonderful husband and money. As hard as I tried not to, I kept thinking about the life and the

146

man I left behind. It was Luke's father Levi Yoder that I loved," she said, her voice trembling with the thought of painful memories.

"So you went back to Levi."

Margaret put her hands behind her back and looked off into the distance. "Not right away. Levi had married another woman, my sister. At that point, there was no reason to go back. But my sister envied my way of life. Not knowing any better, she eventually left Levi and disappeared."

"Then you made up with Levi?"

"No, I was not welcomed in the Amish community in Pennsylvania where we lived. All I asked of Levi was that I be allowed once in a while to see Luke, mine and Levi's son." Hal showed her surprise at that news. "That is another story, I'll save for another time. Anyway since my sister left, the child was without the only mother he had known. Levi agreed to my visits once a year but made it clear he was uncomfortable with me being around. I had been shunned by the Amish community which means that no one, not even my parents, sisters and brothers could talk to me. After awhile, my husband left me, because he realized I did not love him. Levi came to feel he wanted me back in his life. That is when we made up and remarried."

"What a wonderful love story, but how did you get to Iowa?"

"After Levi's father, Jeremiah, died, we sold the farm. My past history had made it hard for Plain people in Pennsylvania to accept me. We did not think they ever would completely. In Iowa, we made a fresh start and were happy." She bent to pull a buttonweed. "Until Levi died last year."

"I'm sorry."

Margaret turned to look her in the eye. "That is the way life is."

"Are you trying to tell me Amish people here may never accept me?"

Margaret advised, "Your story is different from mine. Most of them will find you friendly once they meet you. But

147

there are a few that might make it hard on you. You can be strong and endure or run back to the English way of life."

"Thanks for the advice. I'm not ready to give up yet. The few people I've met do seem to like me. Except for Stella ----," Hal stopped. She darted a questioning glance at the older woman.

Margaret's lips tightened as she nodded. She said, "I think you are beginning to understand me now."

"Do you think she is a real threat to me?"

"Recht now? Jah." Margaret confirmed. "I should not tell this, but I think you ought to know. Stella Strutt has been telling people not to go to your clinic. That is why you have not had patients. You have to get out to meet Plain people so they can judge you for themselves. Stella would not be able to keep up her tales if everyone got to know you."

"How do I do that?"

"Come to Jane Bontrager's quilting bee for starters. I will see what I can do to get you invited to other gatherings. Soon there will be no one left that does not know you for Stella to say negative things to," Margaret planned.

Linda called from the porch, "Come help me with the glasses once."

As they turned back to the house, Hal said, "Thanks for telling me your story. It helps to know I am not alone. On more thing, John tells me if we marry I will have to be submissive to him. If I can't do that, he will not marry me. How did you handle that with Levi?"

Margaret giggled, "Very simple, Nurse Hal. Let the man think he is in charge. After all, he is the head of the household. It is a comfort to know the burdens are on his shoulders. You can get him to see things your way when you need to. It always worked for me."

Hal grinned. "I think I can handle that. As for Stella, she is a force to be reckoned with. She has never liked me. My clinic doesn't stand a thimble full of a chance if she continues to keep people from coming." A thought had Hal concerned, "Helping me will put you in a bad light with her."

Margaret laughed. "I am used to Stella. I do not fear her any more than she does me."

"Well, I do fear her. I unintentionally do things that Stella doesn't approve of," Hal said, looking at John under the tree visiting with his friend.

Margaret saw the glimmer of light in Hal's eyes as she looked at John. "Jah, like your fondness for the Lapp family."

"Yes and Stella is beginning to suspect it," Hal shared.

"I see. John has been a widower for too long. He needs a wife and mother for his children. All the more reason for you to figure out where your heart lies. That is where you will feel at home no matter if you become Amish or stay English," Margaret said approvingly.

"I love John's children. We are like a family already," Hal shared.

"I think that is a gute thing."

Hal shook her head. "I wonder if I'll be able to fill the shoes of Diane Lapp for John and the children. Maybe I shouldn't ask you this, but ----."

"What you say will stay with me."

"I wonder if John's wife was very pretty. What did Diane look like? When I look at Emma, I wonder if she looks like her mother."

"Emma is surely obgagooked."

Hal looked puzzled. "I'm sorry. My Dutch is not very good yet."

"She is the spitting image of her mother," Margaret explained.

"I thought that might be the case," Hal said, looking down at the ground.

"Diane Lapp was sick for a long time. After she died, her death was hard for her family to get over. You are like a breath of spring. You brought them back lavendich." Margaret grinned at Hal's questioning look. "I'm sorry. Lavendich means alive. Never fear about taking her place. You will make your own place in that family. As for mistakes. Everyone makes them. We all have our share of things we wish we had not done. Someone once said failure sometime in your life is inevitable, but giving up is unforgivable. Never give up, Nurse Hal."

Hal gave her a hug. "I really appreciate you telling me this. It makes me feel better."

Later on the ride home, Hal watched the countryside slide slowly by, thinking about all of Margaret's advice. Emma had been right as usual. The scenery was easier to take in at a slower pace. She just wished she could enjoy it. She sighed and laid her head on John's shoulder. If she wasn't so worried, she'd let the buggy's gentle vibration and the rumble of the wheels put her to sleep.

"Why are you so quiet?" John asked, leaning his cheek over on her head.

"Just thinking about my visit with Margaret."

"Did she tell you about being English once?"

With admiration in her voice, Hal said, "She told me the whole story. She's a brave woman to come back to a community that didn't like her and stay because she loved Levi and her son."

"Brave she was."

"Did you know that Stella Strutt is warning people not to come to the clinic?" Hal blurted out.

John see-sawed on the reins, slowed the horse and pulled to a stop on the side of the road. His eyes held a fierce look. "Is that what she is doing?"

"Yes, Margaret says it is. Didn't Elton tell you that when you talked?"

"Nah, I do not think he knows or he would have said something," said John in concern. "What do you want to do about this?"

"Margaret says I should get to as many gatherings as I can like the quilting bees so I meet people. She says if they get to know me, they won't pay any attention to Stella. Do you think that will work?"

"Jah, Margaret is a smart woman. I think it will help. Elton is on your side when it comes to Stella. Should I go see the bishop about this?" He offered.

"Don't bother Elton yet. Let's just wait awhile." She wrapped her arm around John's and snuggled up next to him. "Okay?"

"Okay," he said, meeting her halfway for a long, tender kiss.

Chapter 15

For the next few days, Hal worked up a deep dread about attending Jane Bontrager's quilting bee. She had intended to make up an excuse to keep from going. That was before she knew Stella Strutt was trying to turn the Amish community against her before the Plain people got a chance to know her. She might be able to ignore Stella talking about her behind her back if that was all she did. It wasn't. That woman bad mouthed the clinic John and the others worked so hard to build. Without giving Hal and Emma a chance to help the Amish community, that old, spiteful woman wanted her to give up and go back to Wickenburg. Hal couldn't let that happen. Whether she wanted to or not, she had to stand up to Stella. The best she could hope for was that the crab didn't mow her down and flattened her out like John's hayfield.

So the afternoon of the bee came. Hal was beside Emma in the buggy. They were on their way to the only quilting bee she might ever attend if Stella had her way about it. Hal's lips pressed tightly together with that thought. She didn't really want to go. Quilting in front of other women was a sure way to let them form a bad opinion of her. She was going to be lousy at it. Blast that Stella Strutt for forcing her to stand up for herself. She thought Plain people practiced being pacifists. That meant Hal should hold her temper and be nice to

Stella. She wished Stella would practice her beliefs and do the same. Hal didn't know if she was strong enough to succeed against Stella, but she had to prove to the Amish women that she wanted to live like they did.

Emma looked over at Hal's gloomy face. "You need not worry. The quilting bee will be fun. You'll see."

"Maybe you'll see instead," Hal returned glumly. "Jane's guests will laugh me out of the house once they see how awful I sew."

"They will not," declared Emma.

Hal patted her jean pocket. "Oh, no. I didn't think to bring the thimble you gave me. We should turn around and go home. Oh, that will make us late. Maybe we should just forget about going."

"Take it easy. I have the thimble." Emma patted her dress pocket. "A pair of small scissors for you to cut threat with, too."

"Thanks for thinking of everything. It's a good thing you have your head screwed on straight. I sure don't," Hal grumbled.

Jane Bontrager met Hal and Emma at the door. Women chattering and their laughter reached into the kitchen before the three of them entered the living room. A long quilting frame had been placed in the middle of the room. The row of women on both sides of the tautly stretched quilt reminded Hal of a blue and purple color palette except for Stella Strutt and Margaret Yoder. Those two were dressed in black. A young, round-faced woman sat at a small table at the end of the frame. She was threading needles with white thread and sticking them into strips of cloth.

Nodding toward the woman, Jane introduced her daughter, Amy. "I understand most of these women you already know. Margaret Yoder on this end. On the other side of the two chairs, we saved for you, is Margaret's daughter-in-law, Linda. On the opposite side of the frame across from Margaret here is Roseanna Miller. Next to her is Stella Strutt." All the others gave Hal and Emma a warm smile but not Stella. She scowled ugly enough to wilt Emma's flowers in the garden. "Next is Lizzy Leichenring. The empty chair by her is mine."

"Sit by me, Nurse Hal," Margaret invited. "It is so nice to see you again. How are you?"

"Just fine and you?"

"Gute. Emma, how are you this fine day?" Linda asked.

Emma sat down next to Hal. "I am gute."

"Does this quilt have a name?" Hal asked. She didn't have to glance across the table to see if Stella was glaring at her. Hal could feel the woman's stare, but she wanted to act like she felt comfortable here. Besides if she saw another unfriendly look on that woman's face, she was afraid her pretended calm composure would melt.

Margaret answered, "Jah. It is a wedding ring quilt."

Hal inspected the quilt made from small scraps of material. "Where should I start?"

Margaret instructed, "You can pick any place you want in the ring pattern and sew around the pieces."

Hal glanced around her at what the other women were doing. She slipped on her thimble and placed her scissors on the quilt just like the other women. She drew a threaded needle out of the cloth strip laying on the quilt between Margaret and her. She poised the needle over the material. Sweat beads popped out on her forehead. She dropped her needle and rubbed her palms along her jean legs. Picking the needle up again, she wove it in and out of the quilt three times.

Stella had been watching. Hal knew because the old woman leaned over to Lizzy Leichenring and whispered loudly. "Her stitches look like basting. That woman will ruin this fine quilt."

Hal pulled the needle out and laid it down. All right, Stella meant for her to hear that remark. She intended to meet the old crab's insults head on. She said sweetly, "Tell me, Margaret, are my stitches too big? I want to do this right."

"Perhaps, just a little. Try to make 8 to 10 stitches to an inch." Margaret glanced across at Stella. It was clear she had been listening to Stella, too. "Nurse Hal, we all had to practice

154

to make our stitches smaller. You will be able to do it in time."

"I hope so," Hal assured her, wishing she could get the subject off her stitches. She looked across at Lizzy and asked, "How is David's foot?"

"It has healed. He kept his shoes on for awhile after you talked to him. Just for awhile. He is barefoot again," she said, rolling her eyes toward the ceiling.

Emma laughed. "So are Noah and Daniel. Matter a fact, I like to go barefoot myself."

"Jah," said Lizzy, smiling. "It is better to wait until now when the ground is not so cold."

"Linda and I had such a nice visit with you, Nurse Hal. I hope you come see us again soon," Margaret said.

"Emma, you come along with her," Linda invited.

"We'd love that," Hal said. She kept her head ducked but she sneaked a glance at Stella. The woman's face was beet red. She reminded Hal of a teakettle about ready to blow steam. It would absolutely ruin this quilting bee for all of them if Stella caused a scene and blamed her.

"So Nurse Hal," Stella began, her voice raising on each word. "How is the clinic doing these days." She sounded so smug.

Hal stopped stitching and laid her hands in her lap so Stella couldn't see them shake. "It's nice of you to ask, Stella. The clinic is doing fine. We haven't had any patients lately but that is a gute thing, isn't it? It means everyone around here is healthy."

Very clearly, that wasn't the negative response the woman had hoped to hear. Stella's eyes glared at Hal as if trying to burn a hole through her. Hal felt a zing of revenge. So far she'd managed to keep up with Stella's vindictive attempt to make her look bad in the eyes of the other women.

Without looking up from her stitches, Roseanna offered, "Samuel Nisley had Nurse Hal doctor his arm awhile back. He said she did a fine job. His arm is as gute as new now."

"So is my David's foot," chimed in Lizzy.

Stella puffed up. The lid was about to blow off her imaginary teakettle. Margaret darted a glance at the older woman. With a smile, she laid her comforting hand on Hal's. "Jane, is it about time to prepare us a snack? Stella and I will be very glad to help."

"Jah, it is plenty time. Come with me to the kitchen," Jane said, getting up from her chair.

The buzz that started after the three women disappeared through the kitchen door reminded Hal more of a beehive than a quilting bee.

Darting a look at the kitchen door, Lizzy said in a lowered voice, "I hope you do not think bad of me for saying this but Stella can be crittlich."

Hal leaned toward Emma. The girl whispered, "Crabby."

"The woman is very much a rutz-naus if I can give an opinion," added Linda Yoder.

"Snot nose," Emma translated.

"Oh my," gasped Hal.

Roseanna said, "She is such a hesslich person. I find it hard to like her."

"Hateful," came Emma's whisper.

Hal wasn't sure whether to be happy the women were siding with her or to feel sorry for Stella. She said in a low voice. "Ladies, that seems too harsh to say about anyone."

Linda leaned forward to look around Emma. "We are so sorry for the way crittlich Stella is treating you. Do not think we feel as she does?"

"I understand. I am so glad you don't," Hal told her.

She might have said more if not for what was going on in the kitchen. Margaret's scolding voice carried to the living room, loud and clear. "Sometimes, Stella, I've heard of people who g'warrick'd when they say such bad things about others."

"Choked," Emma whispered.

"It seems I still have a lot of Dutch words to learn. Why haven't you taught me any of these words before?" Hal asked.

"Did not think you would need to know or use these

156

words," Emma said through clenched teeth.

Right after that a door opened and shut. Jane came to the kitchen door. "We have the snack ready. Come to the table and rest for awhile."

Hal filed along behind Emma. Once, they were all seated, Linda asked, "Where is Stella?"

"She went home," Jane said evenly. "Enjoy this chocolate cake once. Nothing is better than chocolate."

As the women chattered away about family, gardens and church, Hal relaxed. The worst was over now. She could enjoy herself. More importantly, the women around the table enjoyed being together now that the large, black damper to laughter and fun had left.

Amish or English, most women must have the same craving for chocolate, Hal thought as she dug her spoon into the cake.

On the ride home, Hal said, "You were right. I had fun, and the quilting bee went better than I could have imagined."

"I am glad you enjoyed it," Emma said seriously. "But I do not know how you thought the quilting bee went well after the way Stella Strutt attacked you."

Hal shook her finger at the girl. "Emma, shame on you! I'm not sure I ever want to know the meaning of that word. What Stella did was make herself look bad to her neighbors. The way she acted backfired on her. Her rude actions caused the women to defend me. I must say I am glad she decided to leave. Everyone perked up after that. I'd say the women were glad when she left."

"The word means vile. I guess you are right. It was gute to see them stand against Stella Strutt. That rarely happens so it must have taken her by surprise," Emma said thoughtfully.

"There is a saying, safety in numbers."

"That may be it. Stella has much more luck bedeviling one person. Not so easy to pick on a crowd," Emma said smiling.

"You got it, my girl."

Emma's smile faded. "I should warn you, Stella has

157

always gotten her own way. She will be thinking up another attack on you. Next time, she will not try it in front of people who have become your friends."

That thought took some of the enthusiasm out of Hal. "One thing Stella Strutt will never be known as is a wishy-washy person when it comes to what she believes. Consider me warned."

"Wishy-washy?"

"She defends what she believes no matter what. Do me a favor?"

"Anything, Hallie."

They were driving by a tree full of crows. The noise of the buggy wheels and the horse hooves made the birds nervous. Cawing sharply several times as a warning, one crow upset the others. The birds circled the tree a couple times and flew away. Just watching those over-sized, noisy, blackbirds made Hal think of Stella Strutt. "If you see Stella Strutt coming before I do will you warn me?"

"Jah," said Emma with a look of dread for what the future held. "And until then, we will see if we can change Stella's mind. Make her a little more wishy-washy."

Chapter 16

When Hal drove in at the Lapp farm the next afternoon, clothes swayed gently on the line behind the clinic. With the coming of warm weather, the gusty, cold blasts of winter leftover wind had turned into gentle, warm caresses that promised summer. Just the right drying conditions to put a fresh smell into laundry.

Noah and Daniel were playing catch near the garden. School was out. The boys had time to play between chores.

In the kitchen, Emma was bustling back and forth to the table. She sat down a plate of cookies on a dishtowel and wrapped the towel around the plate. The table was completely covered with spread out dishtowels, three quart jars of tea and sandwiches.

"What is going on here?" Hal asked.

"We need something to cheer us up and take the taste of Stella Strutt out of our mouths," said Emma. The way she knotted the bundle, with such intensity, made Hal wonder if Emma wanted to do the same thing to Stella.

The boys, racing each other, rushed in and slammed the front door. Daniel made it to Hal first. "Mama Hal, we are going on a picnic."

"Really? What fun," Hal said.

"Really," Noah concurred.

"I can't wait," she said, clapping. "What is your father doing today?"

"He cannot come," Daniel said.

"He is mowing hay today. If he has gute luck, he should be done by chore time." Emma bundled the sandwiches and knotted the dishtowel. "We waited to eat until you got home, Hallie. Now we are starving. We are ready to go."

"Where are we going?" Hal asked.

Daniel giggled. "Where on this farm do you think we would have a picnic?"

"Oh," Hal said and tapped her lips as if that was a hard question. "The picnic grove?"

"Jah," Daniel said, bracing himself on one foot then the other. He was ready to take off.

Emma commanded, "Do not leave until you pick up a bundle, Noah and Daniel. Each of us has to carry food."

The boys grabbed the closest dishtowels and ran for the door.

"They certainly are eager to have a picnic," Hal said, laughing.

"It has been awhile since we have wanted to have fun. I am glad my brothers are looking forward to this," Emma said as she handed Hal a bundle. "Oh, oh, I wonder if Noah forgot to let the horses out of the pen. Daed said the grass is tall enough that they could be turned loose in the pasture now."

Emma grabbed the last bundle and hurried out the door. She pounded down the porch steps with Hal trying to keep up. Her brothers were halfway down the lane to the pasture.

"Noah," Emma yelled.

Noah twisted and yelled back. "What?" He kept walking backward.

Emma cupped a hand around her mouth. "Did you remember to let the horses out this morning?"

Noah and Daniel stopped and looked at each other. Hal couldn't hear what they said, but Noah handed Daniel his bundle and sprinted back toward the barn.

"Guess not," Hal said softly.

"After going to school all day for months, it is hard to get back into the routine at home, but my brothers will. I will see to that." Emma sounded earnestly determined. "Come, Hallie."

Hal didn't know whether to smile or be worried about co-existing in the same house with Emma. For a couple years now, the girl had practiced being the Lapp taskmaster. Since she had quite a bit of experience under her apron strings, Emma was good at it by now. Hal had the feeling she best become a quick learner in regard to being a productive member of this family. If she wasn't, Emma would be a hard taskmaster to her as well.

The pasture grass was tall and lush, hiding most of the pond except for the clear blue middle. A rooster pheasant croaked. Mourning doves answered with coos. The milk cows stopped grazing and lined up to watch the group hike to the picnic grove. Here and there a thistle raised its pink head. Small wild rose bushes covered with pink blooms were scattered about. Larger multiflora rose bushes, full of small white blooms, mingled with the cedar trees. Mullein stalks had turned into bright yellow blooms.

Breathless, Noah caught up beside Daniel. He took his bundle back.

The horses, bucked and snorted, running a race around the pond. The ruckus they made scared a flock of mallard ducks that had been lazily floating on the water. They quacked in protest as they rose with a loud flapping of wings and flew off. The horses straightened and made a lap across the pasture, dodging in and out among various sized cedar trees. They headed right at the cows, scattering them.

"My goodness, look at the horses go. They're glad to be free," said Hal, stopping to watch the four horses.

"That they are," Noah agreed.

Hal put her arm around Noah's shoulder. "Have you ever noticed how different horses are from cows?"

Noah shrugged his shoulders. "No."

"Well, cattle when let out to pasture immediately begin

161

to eat like they're starved when they really aren't. On the other hand, horses don't think about food. They love the feel of freedom and the space to run," observed Hal.

"That is true," said Noah.

"Which would you be if you had a choice, Noah, a horse or a cow?"

"Depends."

"On what?"

"Depends on if I'm hungry or not." Noah grinned at her. "Right now I would be a cow." He glanced at Emma and Daniel entering the trees. "We better catch up. Emma and Daniel are as hungry as us. They intend to eat whether we come or not."

Hal darted off, shouting over her shoulder, "Race you there."

Noah caught up to her and past her as they entered the grove. They dropped down on the ground, trying to get their wind back. Gooseberry bushes, blackberry and raspberry brambles bordered the clearing. All the plants were filled with white blooms. Clusters of May apples with large umbrella shaped leaves mingled among the undergrowth. A small thicket of wild plum trees, in full bloom, made the clearing smell sweet.

Emma, tongue in cheek, said, "If you two are done horsing around we can eat." She handed Hal a sandwich and a cup of tea.

This was the time that Hal had dreamed about and waited for. She loved listening to the children, talking, laughing, scolding, and teasing each other. They felt like hers as sure as if they were born to her. Not quite hers yet, but they would be when John Lapp was legally her husband.

As soon as they devoured the sandwiches, Emma held out the cookie plate. "Ready for some cookies?"

"I'll take two," Hal said.

Noah and Daniel helped themselves. As soon as the boys gobbled down their cookies, Noah said, "I brought the ball. We can play catch, Daniel Lapp."

162

Hal leaned back against a walnut tree and watched the boys race through the trees, headed for the open pasture. "They sure have more energy than I do."

"Me, too," Emma said.

"I've been wondering something. Why do Plain People use both a person's first and last names all the time when they talk to someone or about them?"

Plopping down beside her, Emma crossed her legs Indian fashion and smoothed her skirt. "It is always done that way. You would have to ask Daed to know for sure, but I think the reason is so many Plain people have the same first names and last names. For instance, there might be an Emma Yoder, Emma Miller and Emma Lapp. No one would know which one you were talking about if you did not use both given and last name."

"Makes sense," said Hal, yawning. "Now that my stomach is full, I'm getting sleepy. I think I'm going to go for a walk to wake back up."

"After I get the dishes bundled up, I'll join you," Emma said, gathering the plates and jars.

The picnic grove was a colorful, peace-filled place on this perfect day. As Hal came through the trees, she saw all sorts of wild flowers; delicate, white Dutchman breeches, yellow violets, jack in the pulpit, and several different colors of phlox.

She past two markers. A small one that marked the spot where they had buried their letters to Diane Lapp and a larger one over Patches's grave. She stepped into the open close to the boys. Daniel threw the ball at Noah. Noah missed the catch. As the ball bounced past him in the grass, Hal scooped the ball up and threw it back to him.

"You leaving?" Noah asked, catching the ball.

"Just going to walk off my lunch. Thought I'd like to look at the pond," Hal said.

"Noah replied evenly, "All right."

Daniel, his face strained, warned, "Stay away from the edge so you do not fall in, Mama Hal."

163

"I'll be careful," she assured him.

The large mound of earth called a pond dam ran along one end. From the barn to the pond, a cow path led to a sloped place in the bank, making a beaten, dried mud path to the water. That low spot in the pond, where run-off occurred in rainy seasons, was a jungle of cattails and reeds. Frogs heard her rustling steps in the grass. With grumpy croaks, they jumped high into loud splatting dives, splashing into the green, murky moss covered water along the pond's edge.

The ducks had landed again on the other end of the pond. Busy feeding on plant matter under the water, the ducks had their twitchy tails and padding feet sticking straight up. The noisy frogs got the attention of the mallards. The ducks sat upright and stretched their necks high, quacking softly among themselves. They paddled in a circle, giving her a watchful surveillance.

Hal's shadow fell over the water as she walked across the dam. Small fish darted away from the bank, turning into brief shadows as they dived deeper. When she got as far as the fence that ran close to end of the pond, she turned and started back. Just as she thought. The pond was stocked. A bluegill jumped up. It splashed back under the water, leaving a wake that grew from a small ring to a bigger one as it floated away. Close to the bank, bubbles brewed to the surface as fish fed. One of these days, she wanted to bring the children fishing. Maybe if they thought of this as a place to have fun, they wouldn't always associate the pond with the terrible memories of what happened to their mother.

Soft click-clacks of a horse's hooves seemed close. Hal looked ahead of her. One of the horses was on the dam, headed toward her. The red horse, with a dark red mane, made a blowing snort and nickered quietly, nodding its head up and down.

"Shoo, Ben. Don't come this way," Hal scolded, waving her hands in the air.

The horse nickered again but kept coming.

Hal looked on either side of her. The dam was too

narrow for her to get around that big horse. The fence was behind her and along the dam. She had no place to go.

"Ben, go away," she shouted, clapping her hands to scare him.

The noise didn't work. The horse kept plodding slowly toward her, its head nodding up and down.

"If you're still mad at me, I'm sorry you went in circles. Please stop," Hal begged. She held her hands up, palms out, and darted a glance toward the grove. The boys had disappeared.

"Help!" She yelled. "Help me!" She focused on the horse. "John is going to teach me how to drive better. I promise. Stop now," she ordered, backing up.

The horse kept coming right at her. What was it Samuel said to her? She should have told Ben to whoa when she drove him in circles.

Hal had to stop the horse from trampling her. She yelled, "Whoa."

The horse snorted through flared nostrils as if making fun of her command and kept prodding at her.

Maybe she hadn't been forceful enough. She had to say it like she meant it. She put her hands on her hips and said angrily,

"Whoa, Ben. Whoa." Maybe that horse didn't spook easy, but she sure did. He wasn't listening. Not one word soaked into that stupid horse's birdbrain head. She looked toward the picnic grove and screamed, "Help me."

"We're coming," Noah called, bursting out of the trees.

"Thank goodness," Hal said, backing away from the horse. The fence was close behind her. She had no place else to go. She stopped and waved her hands. "Please, whoa, Ben," she begged.

The horse gave a teeth baring grin and closed in on her. Hal held her hands out in front of her. The horse nudged her palms gently at first with its nose, then gave a harder butt with its head. The force was enough to knock Hal over backward. Flip flopping down the rocky dam, Hal's head connected with

165

a large rock.

Ouch. That hurt, she thought just before she did another head over heels flip and sank into the pond. The cold water was shock enough to keep her from passing completely out. She turned over, sat up in the chest deep water and sputtered to empty her mouth.

The excited chatter of the children came to her as the grass rustled under their running feet. The horse looked down at her and nickered as if laughing at her. Hal tried to focus on him, but all she saw was a mountainous, fuzzy, red blur.

Daniel cried, "OOF!"

"Watch where you are walking. You slipped on a cake of kilrick. Now you will stink," Noah scolded.

"Hurry you two. We need to help Hallie," Emma ordered.

By the time the children peered over the dam at her, Hal was sitting waist deep in water, holding her head. The horse snorted and pawed the dam as if daring her to climb back out while he was watching. Loose rocks and clay chunks rained into the pond, sending small waves of water Hal's way.

Noah grabbed the horse around the neck, turned it around and headed it back along the dam. Following along behind, Daniel slapped the horse's hip. Trotting through the grass, the horse twisted its back end one way than the other. The beast gave a fast kick with both feet high in the air and raced away.

Emma scrambled down the side of the dam. "Hallie, are you all right?"

"Please, do not drown, Mama Hal." Daniel's voice was filled with anguish. His fists were clenched at his sides.

Noah rushed past Daniel. "Help me get her out of the water. She is not going to drown. The water is not deep enough."

Daniel sank to the ground and hugged his knees. Tears ran down his face. "Mama Hal is going to die."

"Noah, I will help you," Emma said as she waded out after him into the water. She touched Hal's temple. "You have

166

a cut on your head, Hallie. Can you stand up?"

"I think so," Hal said, splashing water on the kids as she made an effort to get on her feet. She felt her feet sucked under the mud much like quicksand would do and worried about how deep she would sink. The heavy mud swirled over her tennis shoes, weighing her feet down.

Emma and Noah grabbed Hal's arms to steady her. Together, they waded through the mud riled water.

Listening to Daniel cry, Emma looked toward the dam. "Poor boy, he is really upset."

Hal stopped watching where she was wading. Her heart did a nose dive. The boy's distraught face told her he thought he was going to lose another mother to this pond.

"Stop a minute," Hal whispered. She called to the boy, "Daniel, can you come down to the water and help pull me up the bank?"

"Nah," Daniel sobbed, shaking his head. "Ach, nah, I am scared."

"It is no use, Hallie. He is too afraid," Emma said softly.

"Probably start sleepwalking again already," Noah predicted. "At least, it is warm weather this time."

"I so wanted to bring you kids to fish in this pond. Daniel has to get over his fears if we're going to have fun here," whispered Hal. She called, "Please, Daniel. Our feet are covered with murky mud. The bottom of our shoes are so slick, we won't be able to make it up the dam by ourselves."

Daniel stood up. Slowly because she asked for his help, he headed toward the nightmare he'd had over and over the last two years. He slid down the bank. At the edge of the water, he held his hands out to take Hal's so he could help her.

"I'm really getting tired. Can you come out in the water a little ways to me? I can't quite reach you yet," Hal said, stretching her arms out to him.

Daniel teetered on the edge of the water. His face blanched as he took a step and felt the cold water rush around his leg. He hesitated and looked back up at his safe place on the dam.

"You can do it, Daniel," Hal assured him.

The little boy stuck his other foot in the water. He took a deep breath as the cold water moved against him. Keeping his eyes on Hal's face, Daniel slowly waded to her. He kept his arms stretched out. As soon as he was close enough, Hal took his hands.

"Oh, Daniel, I'm so proud of you for helping me," said Hal, gathering him in her arms.

"Hallie, would it be all right with you if we continue this conversation on dry land?" Emma complained. "This water is cold."

Once they reached the top of the dam, Hal looked around warily. "Where is that mean horse?"

"Do not worry. She has gone to join the others," Noah said.

"Now sit, Hallie," Emma said, helping her down. "How do you feel?"

"Silly for falling into the pond," she said, touching the sore place on her forehead.

"You have a lump coming up fast and a cut. Blood is running down the side of your face. Are you dizzy?" Emma asked.

Pale-faced and worried, Daniel sit down beside Hal and took her hand, wanting to comfort her.

"No, but thanks to that horse we are all soaking wet." She glanced at the children. "Why wouldn't Ben stop? He was bound to dunk me in that pond and nothing I said stopped him."

"That was not Ben," Noah said.

"Was that my problem, I called him the wrong name?"

"The horse is a mare. Her name is Molly. Sometimes, she is a little over friendly," Noah said with a twinkle in his eyes.

"A little over friendly! I wish you had told me about this before I took off on my own. I wouldn't have walked away from your protection if I had known. I gave Molly the perfect opportunity to knock me in the pond," Hal complained.

"She did not do it on purpose," Daniel said, patting her hand. "She likes you."

"Butting me means she likes me!" She saw the quizzical look on the boy's face, and her sense of humor came back. "I'd hate to see how she'd treat me if she didn't like me," said Hal, laughing.

As she walked off the dam, Hal's mud-soaked tennis shoes made a gross sucking sound, squish, squish. The kids paused to look down at her feet. Hal gave her shoes a disgusted glance. "I can't stand these wet shoes. They sound and feel horrible."

"Hallie, sit down and take them off. It is about time you started going barefoot like we do," Emma said with a grin.

Sitting under the maple tree in the house yard, John watched Hal and the children trudge up the pasture lane. Their soaked clothes were plastered to them. Hal was carrying her shoes, wet and mud covered.

Sipping on a glass of tea, his eyes narrowed at the sight in front of him. The closer they came the more puzzled he became. "Oh, my! You are as wet as drowned rats. Go for a swim in the pond?"

"We did," Hal said, winking at Daniel.

"Looks like you picked the mossy end. The west end is a cleaner spot to swim," John suggested, his eyes twinkling.

"Now you tell us," Hal said with mock exasperation.

John noticed blood trickling down the side of Hal's head. He jumped to his feet and turned Hal's face sideways. "Are you all recht?"

"I'm fine. Just connected with a rock."

John sniffed several times. He looked from one to the other and finally focused on Daniel's besmeared, brown stained pant leg. "You do not smell pretty gute, my son."

Noah sniggered. "He fell in a fresh cake of kidrick."

Daniel frowned. He didn't like being the center of attention.

Hal wiped a string of slimy, dried moss from her

169

shoulder. "Not only are we wet, but we brought part of the pond back with us. We have to get out of these clothes and wash up."

"You do not have other clothes here," Emma reminded her.

"No," Hal said. "And wouldn't it be just my luck, Stella Strutt would show up as soon as I put on one of your mother's dresses?" Hal's eyes brightened. "Wonder what she'd say if she caught me in your father's shirt and pants?"

"You need to be dry so maybe we better risk finding out,"

Emma said. "While we're at it, I need to clean that cut on your head."

"Wait a minute. Are you going to ask me if you can borrow my clothes?" John asked with a crooked grin.

"Oh, I'm sure you won't mind. You'd hate to see me catch a cold. Besides, while Emma lays out your clothes in the spare room for me, you and I need to have a talk about the rude manners of your horse named Molly."

Chapter 17

Days later, Hal watched the capacious, summer clouds scud across the bright blue sky from the clinic window. Her spirit felt light enough to ride on one of those clouds. Most of the problems in her life had resolved themselves. Emma had helped her finish the wedding dress and one of the everyday dresses was almost done. Soon she would have her Amish wardrobe to wear when the time was right.

The biggest obstacle to her marrying John was the meeting with the bishop. She felt confident that would go well. Emma had been a good teacher. Hal could now stutter her way through enough Dutch to pass Bishop Bontrager's inspection. Even words used in anger thanks to Stella Strutt. Not that she intended to use any of those words around the bishop. In spite of herself, Elton Bontrager liked her. She wanted to keep it that way.

She still had the nine classes of indoctrination to do, and she was eager to get them out of the way. As soon as she was bapisted into the church, John could have their marriage announced at a church meeting. Two weeks after the announcement, they would be able to have the ceremony.

Stella Strutt, no doubt, would have something to say about John Lapp marrying an English woman. Especially this wild redhead. She wasn't a woman to give up when she believed she was right. Right now, Stella's sights were on keeping the Amish community from using the clinic, thinking that would get rid of her. Sometimes, Hal felt as if she was wasting her time, waiting for patients. Maybe Stella Strutt had already done too much damage to her repetition.

Running a fingertip along the edge of the table, Hal pictured what it would be like to have a steady stream of patients. Unfortunately, that wasn't going to happen as long as Stella had so much influence over the Amish community. Hal didn't intend to give up. Not by a long shot was she going to let Stella win this battle or any other if she could help it. Hal firmly believed the day would come when Stella's cruel words about her wouldn't carry any weight. As Emma so often said, Hal just had to have patience.

Hal heard the rustle of feet. John was standing in the clinic doorway, grinning at her like a cat that ate a canary. She looked at the happiness on his face and in his chocolate eyes and knew she should be smiling, too. This day and the days to come were too full of promise to keep going over bad thoughts. Thoughts of Stella were definitely a downer she didn't need to ruin her day.

Hal stood up and leaned against the table. "Hello, sir. What can I do for you today? Have a splinter in your finger? Maybe a sprained ankle I can tape up?"

"Afraid not. I am as healthy as a horse," chuckled John.

"Don't get me started on the condition of your horses, Mr. Lapp," Hal said, laughing.

Something was going on in the house beyond the clinic door. The children's excited voices led her to think something was up. She darted John a questioning look. He gave her a grin in return. "John, spill the beans. What is going on in there?"

"Come with me," he said.

Hal followed him through the living room to the kitchen. They stopped at the doorway. Covered with dish towels, the table was filled almost as full of supplies as the day she'd gone with the children on the picnic. Emma hummed as she tied the bundles shut.

Hal put her hand on John's shoulder. "What's happening?"

John stuffed his hands into his trousers pockets. "We are going camping."

"How fun! Where?"

"The picnic grove. Noah, did you bring your wagon up by the back door?" John asked.

"Yes."

"Start filling it," Emma instructed. She gave Hal a hug. "I would not have believed a wish on a rainbow could come true, but yours did."

"If that's true, the next rainbow I see I intend to make another wish," Hal said amused.

"I might should warn you not to press your luck, but what will you wish for?" Emma asked.

"Don't know. I need to give that some thought," Hal mused. "When I decide I'll tell you. You and I can wait to see if my wish comes true together."

John grabbed her hand and led her outside. They walked down the lane holding hands, John pulling the wagon. It was stacked high with dish towel bundles.

"So you wish on rainbows," John said.

"Sure, doesn't everyone?" Hal asked, grinning at him. She looked back at the house. Emma waved at them from the porch. "Aren't the children coming?" Hal asked.

"Nah."

Hal stopped walking. The realization of what was taking place hit her. "You mean it's just going to be you and me," she squeaked.

John dropped the wagon tongue. It clattered as it hit the packed ground.

There he goes again, shoving his hands in his pant pockets, Hal thought as she waited for his explanation.

John stared at her, his chocolate brown eyes brimming with a loving warmth. No other man had ever looked at her like that before. "Jah. Is that all recht?"

Hal hesitated. This move was so sudden. She had to

173

think about this camping trip and what she wanted to happen next. No children. A private time alone with John Lapp. Marriage close to happening. Why wouldn't spending the night with John be all right?

She saw the way John watched her. His eyes filled with love and now concern. That look made her heart feel like it might bounce out of her chest. John intended to wait patiently for her to make up her mind. A plain, simple man who questioned what her answer would be now that she'd figured out what was in store for her.

The freshly mowed hayfield gave off a pleasant odor of drying alfalfa. The setting sun threw a red streak of fiery light across the pond. The picnic grove trees loomed above the pasture grass, waving in the breeze as if beckoning them to keep coming.

"It's a lovely evening for camping. Sure, I'll come if you want me," she said, shrugging her shoulders.

"You know the answer to that," he said quietly.

"Is it that simple?" She asked wistfully.

In one swift movement, John stepped over the wagon tongue. Gently, he framed her face in his hands. "Jah. That simple if you love me."

"I do love you."

John picked up the wagon tongue, took her hand again and continued his slow march to the grove.

As they crossed the pasture, Hal glanced all around her, nervous about being in this open stretch of grass. "Where are the horses?"

"You are safe while you are with me," John said, looking serious. "Always," he added.

"That's a great comfort, John," she said, squeezing his hand.

John grinned at her nervousness. "The horses are shut in their pen for the night."

"Good, I don't want another run-in with Molly just yet," Hal said.

As dusk set in, a gossamer mist rose from the pond as

the chill of night met the warmth of day. A blue heron stalked into the cattails to hide. The annoying gnats Hal had battled during the day disappeared. A buzzing whine near her arm told her a lonely mosquito was coming in for a landing. Good thing there was a breeze. Otherwise, she'd be fighting more than one before they built the campfire.

Very clearly, someone had been to the picnic grove before them. If Hal had to make a guess, she would say Emma and the boys prepared the clearing for this overnight camp out. Sticks of wood piled in a rick were supported between two hickory nut trees. In the middle of the clearing, a ring of rocks was filled with a pile of sticks for a campfire.

Three wood blocks had been stood and lined up just beyond the rock ring. On the middle one was Emma's vase, covered with painted red roses and blue forget-me-nots. It was chocked full of Queen Anne's lace, black-eyed Susans and wild fern leaves. The blocks on either side of the vase held glass candle holders with a white tapered candle in each. This camping trip had been planned ahead of time down to the littlest detail all right. She thought about Emma humming as she tied the bundles. Oh yeah, the name Emma comes to mind. This is her doing.

It was just turning from dusk to dark as John squatted down to light the fire.

Hal pointed to the candles. "Let me guess. Emma's doing."

Spreading a blanket out in the grass, John nodded, "She said English people think candles are important at times like these."

"They are in a romantic English setting, but I don't think candle light can beat a campfire in a romantic Amish setting," said Hal, giggling.

"Just the same, I have to light the candles. Emma would be beside herself if I brought them back unused," John declared.

A chorus of bull frogs sang a deep, bass song on the pond bank. The pond was close, but with that many voices, the frogs sounded loud enough to be hiding behind the trees with the peepers. Crickets, in the grass, were just about as loud. A dry limb cracked somewhere just beyond the fire light. Hal tensed and strained to hear. She grabbed John's arm. "Something is out there!"

"Jah," he said calmly. "All sorts of animals call the picnic grove home. We are the uninvited guests."

"Like what kind of animals?" Hal asked, squinting to see in the brush around them.

John hunted through the food bundles in the wagon as he listed, "Coons, skunks, possums or a cat hunting for a field mouse."

Hal grimaced at the thought of mice trying to smuggle into their camp. "I don't do good around mice. Any chance any of those critters will try to run us off?"

"Nah. We are bigger than they are," John said. The corners of his mouth twitched as he watched her search around the clearing. Finally, she got tired of beating the bushes with a limb and sat down on the blanket.

Suddenly, Hal looked worried about John going through the bundles. "What did Emma put in for supper? I can't cook very gute you know."

"Emma sent along sandwiches and cookies. Popcorn, too. No cooking tonight."

"Oh good. I love popcorn. Can we start with that first?" She paused then came up with a new worry. "What about breakfast?"

"We have eggs, lard and a skillet. Eggs are not hard to fry," John assured her.

"No, guess I can manage that." One worry seemed to lead to another one in her head. When she was nervous, she always fretted. She didn't think she'd ever be able to change that. "What am I going to do, John? I depend on Emma for so much. One of these days she's going to grow up and marry. How long do I have to learn to cook before she leaves us?"

John brought a bundle over and sat down by her on the blanket. "Emma will be baptized into the church at eighteen.

She can date, but women usually wait until they are twenty to choose a husband."

"At least, five years. Maybe that will be enough time," Hal said doubtfully. She wasn't certain.

"Enough worrying about Emma and cooking." John leaned toward her to kiss her. Hal was watching the bushes on the other side of the fire. He had to say her name softly to get her attention. "Hal."

The campfire flames danced in the night air, casting long shadows over his face. The flame of the candles flickered as they grew long and then short, depending on the breeze. The evening was sweet and mellow. In the distance, whippoorwills cried to each other. On the pond bank, bullfrogs still croaked their long rumbles. Fireflies darted here and there, lighting the dark with tiny glowing beacons.

How much more romantic could this night get? Hal thought as she leaned toward John to collect that kiss.

A series of shrill, high pitched yips carried from the rim of the hayfield ridge behind the grove. Hal snatched John's arm and dug her fingernails into his shirt sleeve. Her eyes widened as she screeched, "What is that?"

"A pack of coyotes," he said, removing her tight grip from his arm.

Somewhere in the underbrush came a wild, fierce, blood-thirsty, bone-chilling squall like scream.

Hal jumped out of her skin and came up on her knees. "John, that animal sounds fierce. What is that awful thing?"

Taking advantage of her nervousness, John dug at the dirt with a stick as he said, "Could be a mountain lion."

"A mountain lion? Have you seen one around here?" She gave him a doubtful look.

"No, but Amos Muhlenberg has seen tracks on his land," John said evenly.

"How far away does Amos live?"

John scratched the side of his head. "Fifteen miles from here."

"Great! Is that all?" Hal said sarcastically as she ran for

the wood pile. She gathered up an arm load of sticks and rushed back to the campfire. She threw the wood into the flames and turned to go for more.

"Whoa, Hal. Mind not putting any more wood on the fire. The kids will think we have set the grove on fire and come to rescue us. One thing I do not want tonight is for my kids to join us." John got up and moved the blanket farther away. "Besides, I feel like a side of pork roasting on a spit already." He plopped down again. Taking his hanky out of his back pocket, he wiped his sweaty face.

"Fine, I'll let that old lion get you," Hal snapped.

She twirled around and tromped out of the trees. She didn't go too far before she sat down Indian fashion in the pasture. Faced with the pitch black night, she darted a look one way then the other. Suddenly, she wondered how smart she had been to leave the protection of John and a blazing fire. It might be her instead of John the mountain lion got out here in the open. A sliver of orange moon peeked above the horizon, ready to join the mass of stars twinkling in the black velvet sky. As Hal watched the moon come out of hiding, she heard the whisper of grass cease. John was standing behind her.

"Come sit beside me," she invited, thinking if she had to die he might as well go with her for bringing her camping among so many wild animals. John had to know dangerous animals prowled the grove at night. What was he thinking when he picked here to camp out? They would have been a lot safer in the front yard or the barn.

As Hal put her hand on his chest, she felt John's beard tickle her skin. "Isn't that moon something? It must be an owl moon."

"What makes you think that?" John asked, putting his hand over hers.

"Noah told me that's what to call a full moon." High up in one of the walnut trees, an owl hooted five times. "See I told you it was an owl moon."

John laughed. "Nah, Noah needs some more information. An owl moon is in February when the owls are looking for a mate. I must admit though I feel like hooting right now to see if it works."

"Oh," Hal said quietly.

John's voice sounded troubled. "Are you upset with me? I did not mean to hurt your feelings. The noise we heard was a very tiny screech owl not a mountain lion."

"You should be careful about teasing me," she warned.

"I see that," he said huskily. "Maybe we should call tonight's moon John's moon since the owl has no right to claim it this time of year."

"Oh, John, are you sure you know me well enough to want to put up with me?"

"You do surprise me when I least expect it, but I am quick to bounce back. I think the way you are is why I love you. Besides, you should know I can duck when I have to," he said, chuckling

"Well, for your information I'm not mad at you. I'm nervous," Hal whispered, keeping her eyes on the moon. Higher in the sky, the circle of light was some smaller and white except for the dark shadows of craters. "Can you fix that for me, Mr. Lapp?"

"I'll give it a good try. There is another old saying. Courage is fear that has said its prayers. Have the courage to come to me, Hal, and your fears will blow away in the wind." He put his hands in her hair and pulled her gently to him. Not for the run of the mill, the children might be watching, peck type kiss, but a long, lingering kiss that felt like it was going to knock Hal's socks off.

After that kiss, she didn't hear the frogs, mice, whippoorwills or that weird little owl anymore. She even forgot about the night roaming mountain lions and coyotes that might come into the camp uninvited to attack them. John would take care of her and protect her. After all, he did say he was supposed to be the boss in this family. When it came to fighting off wildlife, Hal intended to make him keep his word. Before morning, they might just find out how good his word was. They had the whole night ahead of them.

About The Author

Fay Risner lives with her husband on a central Iowa acreage along with their chickens, rabbits, goats and cats. A retired Certified Nurse Aide, she now divides her time between writing books, livestock chores, working in her flower beds, the garden and going fishing with her husband. Fay writes books in various genre and languages – historical mystery series, Stringbean western series, Amish series set in southern Iowa and books for Caregivers about Alzheimer's. She uses 12 font print in her books and 14 font print in her novellas to make them reader friendly. Now her books are in Large Print. Her books have a mid western Iowa and small town flavor. She pulls the readers into her stories, making it hard for them to put a book down until the reader sees how the story ends. Readers say the characters are fun to get to know and often humorous enough to cause the readers to laugh out loud. The books leave readers wanting a sequel or a series so they can read about the characters again.

Enjoy Fay Risner's books and please leave a review to make others familiar with her work.

Other Books By Fay Risner

Nurse Hal Among The Amish Series
A Promise Is A Promise   Doubting Thomas
The Rainbow's End   Amish Country Arson
Hal's Worldly Temptations
Second Hand Goods   As Her Name Is So Is Redbird
Emma's Gossamer Dream   The Courting Buggy
Joyful Wisdom

Amazing Gracie Historical Mystery Series
Neighbor Watchers   Poor Defenseless Addie
Specious Nephew   Will O Wisp
The Country Seat Killer   The Chance Of A Sparrow
Moser Mansion Ghosts Locked Rock, Iowa Hatchet Murders
The Wayward Preacher   Who Killed The Schoolmarm

Westerns
Stringbean Hooper Westerns   Tread Lightly Sibby
The Dark Wind Howls Over Mary   The Blue Bonnet-novella
Small Feet's Many Moon Journey   A Coffin To Lie On-novella
Ella Mayfield's Pawpaw Militia-Civil War

Christmas books
Christmas Traditions - An Amish Love Story
Christmas With Hover Hill   Leona's Christmas Bucket List

Fiction
Listen To Me Honey – novella
Cowboy Girl Annie -novella   Jacob's Spirit – novella
Robot Grandma – novella
Katrina's Gift – novella
Haunted Teapot On Whistler Street -novella

Children Books
Spooks In Claiborne Mansion
My Children Are More Precious Than Gold
Mr. Quacker
Nonfiction about Alzheimer's disease
Open A Window - Caregiver Handbook
Hello Alzheimer's Goodbye Dad-author's true story
Renee Brown Mystery Series
The Answering Machine Knew - novella
One Big Bat – novella   Crystal's Beau-novella
Innocent Until Proven Guilty - novella

181

If you have enjoyed book two in the series about Nurse Hal next is book three Hal's Worldly Temptations. Here is the synopsis for that book.

Join the fun. You are invited to the wedding of John Lapp and Nurse Hal. Family and friends have gathered to cook, clean and plan. Men have put up a tent for the guests, so put on your bonnet or felt hat, hitch up your buggy and take a ride by scenic pastures and rolling hills to Wickenburg, Iowa. Take a seat on a bench next to Hal's folks. They will be glad to explain the ceremony because they came armed with Aunt Tootie's book on Amish customs. You will find a few surprises when little Daniel Lapp interrupts the bishop when he asks if anyone objects to the couple's marriage. Oh, and Stella Strutt has some sort of fit. It will be the most talked about Amish wedding for years to come. Hal's married life is downhill from there. She refuses to give up her car and cell phone. Getting caught by Stella Strutt at the Old Thrasher Reunion on a "joy ride" doesn't help her avoid punishment. Is Hal going to get sent away before she gets settled in? Stick around after the wedding and find out, why don't you?